A BASKET FULL OF BABIES

BOOK THREE OF THE NIGHTINGALE FAMILY SERIES

FENELLA J. MILLER

Boldwood

First published in 2017 as *Better Bend Than Break*. This edition first published in Great Britain in 2024 by Boldwood Books Ltd.

Cover Design by Colin Thomas

Cover Photography: Colin Thomas

A CIP catalogue record for this book is available from the British Library.

Paperback ISBN 978-1-83518-703-6

Large Print ISBN 978-1-83518-702-9

Hardback ISBN 978-1-83518-701-2

Ebook ISBN 978-1-83518-704-3

Kindle ISBN 978-1-83518-705-0

Audio CD ISBN 978-1-83518-696-1

MP3 CD ISBN 978-1-83518-697-8

Digital audio download ISBN 978-1-83518-698-5

Boldwood Books Ltd
23 Bowerdean Street
London SW6 3TN
www.boldwoodbooks.com

1

COLCHESTER, OCTOBER 1844

Her name was Sarah Cooper – she could hardly believe she was no longer a Nightingale like her brother Alfie. She twisted the thin gold band around her finger and smiled shyly at her husband.

'Well, Sarah love, you've made me the happiest of men.' He didn't kiss her but pulled her hand through the crook of his arm and led her back down the aisle.

'I can't remember ever being so happy, Dan, and to think that only two years ago...'

'No, lovey, put the past behind you. You're my wife now, ma to our three boys, and it's my job to look after you all.'

She emerged from the church just as the heavens opened. Was this a bad omen? Then the children threw themselves at her and she forgot her silly fears.

'Are we going to get wet, Ma?' Joe, the eight-year-old, asked as he danced around clinging on to her hand.

''Fraid so, son, but it's not far from the church to our house. If we all run it won't be too bad,' Dan said as he ruffled the boy's hair.

The youngest, John, held out his arms to be picked up. 'You're a bit too big to be carried, young man, and we can run faster holding hands.'

'Yes, Ma, I'm the bestest runner.'

Davie, almost as tall as his brother although he was a year younger, grabbed John's other hand. 'We're blocking up the doorway, Ma. We'd better set off.'

Dan took the lead with Joe close beside him; she raced along behind holding her skirts up with her left hand and clutching Davie's with the other.

The weather had been clement when they had set out to St Leonard's Church but the clouds had rolled in whilst they were inside exchanging their vows.

Dan already had the door open and they tumbled in laughing and shaking the rain from their clothes and hair.

'Joe, stay by the door so you can open and close it when anyone arrives,' Dan said. 'Would you look at that – blooming rain's stopped now. We could have waited and saved ourselves a deal of bother.'

'Never mind,' Sarah said, 'at least our guests won't get wet. It's a good thing we didn't put out any of the food before we left or it would have been quite spoiled.'

'You get the kettle on, love, and I'll get the boys to start taking out the sandwiches and cakes. I still think we should have had some beer to celebrate the occasion.'

The front door opened and shut and her brother Alfie and her best friend Betty Thomas burst in laughing. They seemed a bit too cosy to her. Alfie was only sixteen and in her opinion far too young to be courting.

It was different for her – she had married an older man, someone with a good job who could take care of her and the boys. Alfie had done well for himself in London, come back with his pockets full, but he wasn't properly established in Colchester as yet and must be living on his savings.

'You should have waited a bit, Sarah. The rain stopped and the rest of us have walked here without getting wet.' Alfie was a head taller than her and looked older than his years.

'Don't just stand there; you and Betty have jobs to do. I'm the bride – I shouldn't have wait on you and everyone else today.'

Betty hugged her and dashed into the kitchen and Sarah heard her put the kettle on the range. The mugs, milk jug, teapots and sugar were all waiting. All that had to be done was to boil the water and tip it in.

Dan joined her in the front parlour where they had decided to greet the guests as they came in before directing them outside. 'Is the backyard very mucky after that rain? Do you think we should stay in here?'

'Don't fret, sweetheart; no one will mind getting a bit of dirt on their boots. The boys are wiping down the benches and chairs so they won't be wet to sit on.'

'I can hear others arriving. I wish my ma could have been here to see me wed.'

He squeezed her shoulder and she wiped away the unwanted tears. Nothing was right about this marriage. Although she loved the children and was very fond of Dan, theirs wasn't going to be a proper marriage – at least not for the moment.

All his mates, and their families, from the timber yard crowded into the small house as well as Mr and Mrs Davies, and a dozen or so other friends of Dan's. She and Betty had made plenty of food so no one would go hungry. In pride of place, on the trestle that served as a table, was the cake. She had made this herself and was proud of her efforts – she hoped it tasted as good as it looked.

Halfway through the afternoon Mrs Davies drew her to one

side. 'Sarah, lovey, I reckon one of the menfolk went to a beer-house and brought back a few jugs.'

'I thought the noise was getting louder. There's nothing I can do about it. I just thought with so many children attending my wedding breakfast that alcohol wasn't a good idea.'

The front door had been left open to allow a welcome breeze to drift through the house. There was no danger that uninvited visitors would come in as Alfie's huge dog, Buster, was guarding the opening. It would be a brave person who tried to step past him.

The dog barked and she stepped back into the passageway to see what had disturbed him. 'Good heavens, Ada, I'm so glad you have come after all.'

Ada Billings had taken her in when she had been all but desti-tute and Sarah had kept in touch with her. 'Come out of the way, Buster; let my guests come in.' The dog heaved himself to his feet and stood there, waist-high, his long grey tail wagging.

'I hope you don't mind, I brought my oldest son, Robert, with me. He's a pal of your Alfie and has just got back from Harwich after his last voyage.'

'Have you not brought any of the children? There are more than a dozen playing in the yard with my three boys.'

'No, bless you, you wouldn't want my brood racketing about at your wedding breakfast. The neighbour's keeping an eye out for them so I can't stay long.'

Her son was tall, had broad shoulders, a pleasant face and startlingly bright red hair. He held out his hand and she shook it. 'I'm delighted to meet you, Mrs Cooper. Alfie has told me so much about you I feel we're friends already.'

'Please call me Sarah – everyone else does. Come in. The tea and ginger beer are in the kitchen and I'm pretty sure there's beer available in the yard.'

Robert smiled and wandered off – she wasn't surprised he'd ignored the tea and ginger beer. 'Ada, you look so much better. I can't believe the difference in you since I saw you a few months ago.'

'I told Billings there would be no more babies in my house and if he wanted a bit of how's your father he'd have to find it somewhere else. He's moved in with his fancy woman in Barrack Street and good riddance to him. My Robert is taking care of us now.' She beamed proudly. 'He's going up in the world you know, is taking exams and everything. I reckon he'll be a captain of a ship before he's finished.'

'He's a cut above his brother and pa, then? I didn't know the sons of ordinary folk like us ever got to be a captain of a ship. I'm pleased for you – your life will be so much easier from now on.'

A sudden burst of laughter outside interrupted their conversation. Sarah led the way into the yard to see what was causing all the commotion.

'Good heavens, they're playing the Reverend Crawley's game. I'm going to join in,' Sarah said, and ran across to take her place in the circle. The object of this game was to join hands with the people in the ring, but you couldn't hold the hand of anyone standing beside you.

She found herself attached to Robert Billings with her right hand and an unknown child with her left. It took a considerable time for everyone who wanted to play to get themselves in position. Now the fun started as the object was to untangle themselves without letting go.

She couldn't remember laughing so much in her whole life and when eventually the knot was undone to her astonishment she discovered there were two separate circles of players, one inside the other.

Dan put his arms around her and she leant back into his embrace. He rested his chin on top of her head and sighed.

'Is something wrong?'

'No, my love, I couldn't be happier. When everyone's gone, I need to show you something. Alfie and Betty are going to take care of the boys whilst we're out for a bit.'

* * *

'Do you know why Dan wants us to look after the kiddies?' Betty asked as she collapsed into a chair with a mug of tea and a slice of wedding cake.

Alfie did know, but it wasn't his place to tell Betty. It wouldn't be right if she knew before his sister. 'No idea, Betty love. As long as I can sit here with me feet up I don't care how long they're out.' He was on his third, or maybe fifth, mug of beer and was feeling everything was right in his world. He gestured towards the three boys, his nephews now he supposed, who were playing with a wooden fort and a dozen or so lead soldiers.

'I like the little lads – they're no trouble. What time do you have to be back at Grey Friars?' Betty was an under nurse at a grand house at the top of East Hill, the job she'd taken over after Sarah and then Sally had got the sack.

'I told you, cloth ears, I have to be home before ten o'clock. Dan said he would have Sarah back here long before it's time to put the boys to bed.'

The youngest child began to whine and immediately she was on her feet and smoothing things over. He watched her and couldn't help smiling at his good fortune. He had a tidy sum in the bank, two boys working for him doing deliveries with his barrows and he had more than enough orders for tables, beds, bookcases and dressers to keep him busy until spring.

On top of that, he'd met Betty. She was a bit older than him, but that didn't make no never mind. She had set her cap at him and no mistake. If he didn't want to find himself leg-shackled he'd better do something about it sharpish.

He'd been careful to stay out of her drawers, although he'd been tempted several times. If he got her in the family way he'd have no choice but to marry her and he wasn't sure, despite the fact that she was a pretty little thing and mad for him, that she was the one for him.

The squabble settled, Betty returned to her chair. 'I think Sarah looked ever so pretty, didn't she, Alfie? Her gown and bonnet were her wedding present from Dan.' She put her mug down so sharply the tea slopped onto the table. 'I gave her some handkerchiefs that I'd embroidered. What did you give her?'

'You'll find out soon enough. Wait until they get back from their walk.'

He would have been content to sit quiet, listening to the birds in the trees and the childish chatter at the far end of the yard, but Betty wasn't one for long silences.

'You know where they've gone, don't you? You're a sly one, Alfie Nightingale, keeping secrets from your intended like this.'

He put his beer down and tried to gather his thoughts, which were a bit all over the place owing to the amount of beer he'd consumed during the afternoon.

'I think you've got a bit ahead of yourself, love. I don't remember asking you to marry me. We ain't engaged or nothing – just walking out, as far as I'm concerned.'

He expected her to make a fuss, but instead she smiled and nodded. 'I was just teasing, seeing if you were listening after all that beer you and the other blokes drank.'

'That's all right then. Don't want any misunderstandings on

that score. I'm fond of you, love, but I'm not ready to settle down for a good while yet.'

'And neither am I. I want to save for my bottom drawer before I think of getting wed. There's something I want to ask you, Alfie, about that Mr Hatch.'

'What about him?'

'I've heard things about him and none of them good. You don't want to get in too deep with a man like that.'

'I don't take to him myself – he's a nasty bit of work. But he's a good customer and I can't afford to turn away his trade. When I'm properly established I won't need to deal with the likes of him.' This was something that worried him too. 'I want to find meself a house with a decent backyard where I can work, but he's my land-lord so I can't offend him at the moment.'

Buster nudged him with his long nose and whined softly. 'All right, all right, old fellow, I'll take you for a walk along the river. He's been good as gold all day. He deserves to have a run-around before you go home.'

'You go, Alfie love; I'll finish tidying up here.'

There was no need for him to slip the rope around the dog's neck – the animal never left his side until he gave him leave to do so. However, he always took it with him just in case. The tide was in and the wharf was busy. Whenever he saw the red sails of a Thames barge his stomach churned.

It seemed a lifetime ago that he'd been gullible enough to hop onto a barge thinking he'd found himself a job and was then sold into slavery on a coal lighter on the Thames. If he saw the bastard again he'd be tempted to knock him into the river, but knew he wouldn't do it. He didn't know if Black Ben, the bloke what bought him, still had legal rights – Buster had been his dog and the peelers could still do him for theft.

He walked past the timber yard where Dan worked as foreman and where Alfie bought his timber to make his furniture. It was a bugger pushing the carts up Hythe Hill full of wood – what he needed was a house this end of town.

'Go on, Buster, catch us a rabbit.' The dog rushed off into the water meadows that edged the Colne, leaving him to stroll along the river wall enjoying the early evening sunshine. He'd made his fortune in London and lost the best friend he'd ever had – he hadn't liked the smoke and smog of the city and had vowed never to leave the countryside again.

He had a feeling that from today his life, like Sarah's, would change for the better.

* * *

'Where are you taking me, Dan? Why are we going over the bridge towards Greenstead?'

'Patience, Sarah love. I've got something to show you and it's another half a mile.'

'I can't tell you how much I enjoyed today. We put on a good spread and everyone had a jolly time. We mustn't be too long – John will be needing his bed in an hour or so and Betty told me she wants to spend a few hours alone with Alfie before she has to return to Grey Friars.'

'I reckon your friend intends to marry your brother. Would you mind if she did?'

'I'm not sure. I don't think so. Anyway, he's got more sense than to get her into trouble; he told me only the other day he doesn't want to get married until he's older. Sixteen years of age is too young, if you want my opinion.'

'You Nightingales are a different lot to everyone else, sweetheart. You both have old heads on young shoulders – I wouldn't have asked you to marry me if I thought you weren't ready for it.'

A flicker of something – she wasn't sure what – made her tense. Immediately he patted her hand. 'Don't worry, sweetheart, I'm not going back on my word. You won't have to share my bed until you want to.'

They were in the country now, surrounded by open fields, and the smell of the drains that hung over The Hythe all summer was absent here. He stopped and pointed to a row of pretty cottages that all stood separate and had a decent bit of land surrounding them.

Now she understood why they had come here. 'Have you taken one of those for us? Are we going to live in Greenstead?'

'If you don't mind a bit of a walk to do your shopping, love, then we are. Come on, I'll show you the house I've bought for you.'

'We don't rent it? I didn't know I'd married a rich man, Dan Cooper.'

'I don't own it outright, love, but I've put down a fair bit and will pay off the rest each month. Only the best is good enough for my bride.'

They crossed the Greenstead Road, dodging past the diligences and carts on their way to Wivenhoe and Brightlingsea, and hand in hand they ran to the front gate of what was going to be their new home.

The front garden, if you would call it this, was a scrubby patch of grass with a barely discernible path leading to the front door. This had once been green, but was now in a sad condition.

'I know it doesn't look much at the moment, lovey, but with a lick of paint and a bit of hard work I'll soon have it right.'

He produced a large rusty ring upon which were two big keys

and two slightly smaller. Sarah held her breath as he inserted a large one into the lock and turned it. 'I'll have to give it a shove with my shoulder; it sticks a bit,' Dan said and then with a little help from him the door flew open, catapulting them both into the dark and musty interior.

'It's been empty for a bit. The last tenants did a runner and the landlord hasn't been able to find anyone else who fit the bill. That's why he was pleased I bought it and he'd not have to rent it out again.'

The flagstone entrance hall could do with a good scrub, and the limewash on the walls needed replacing, but apart from that it didn't look too bad.

'I'm going to open the back door and let a bit of sunlight and air in so we can see properly.' He strode down the narrow passageway that bisected the house and after a bit of shoving light flooded in.

'That's much better, Dan, thank you. I like the way the house is divided. I want to see the kitchen first. I don't expect it's got such a good range as we have already.'

'Don't worry about that – I'm getting it moved here. It doesn't belong to the landlord and I've got the old grate in the shed and will put that back in before we leave.'

He opened the door on the left and Sarah peered around his shoulder. 'This doesn't look too bad; in fact it looks really...' She stopped and flung her arms around his neck. 'This is what you and Alfie have been up to these past weeks. The dresser, table, shelves and cupboards have all been made by my brother, haven't they?'

He hugged her back. 'They are our wedding present to you. I paid for the timber and Alfie made them. That's not all – come and look in the front parlour and then upstairs.'

The front room was to the right of the front door and bigger than the one they had at the moment. This had, like the kitchen, been scrubbed and freshly limewashed. In here there was a handsome dresser, two smaller tables and a wooden settle just crying out for her to make a padded seat. The windows looked out on the front garden and the road. The paintwork on these was freshly done as was everything else in here.

'You left the hall as it was deliberately to fool me. This is the best wedding present I could have had; and you're the best husband and Alfie's the best brother. I didn't think my wedding day could get any better, but it has.'

He put his arm around her waist and squeezed, and dropped a kiss on her cheek. 'We painted everywhere apart from the hall. Come and see the other rooms.'

There was a second sitting room, one that they could use every day, on the left. Behind the front parlour was a scullery with a laundry copper, and a large stone sink.

'Give the pump handle a go, Sarah. You'll get fresh water from the well straight into the sink.'

She did as he suggested and was thrilled to find she had water directly into the house and would no longer have to go out into the yard to collect it.

'I take it that's the privy – but why does it have such a large door?'

'It's a family one, one large seat and one small.'

She laughed. 'The boys can go in together, but I can assure you I shan't be taking any of them in with me when I go.' She pointed to a freshly built chicken coop at the far end of the substantial plot. 'We can have more chickens now – and I can see what looks like the outline of a vegetable plot too. Would you mind if I grow flowers as well? I've always wanted hollyhocks, lupins and maybe Michaelmas daisies as well.'

'The garden is your domain, love; you do what you like with it. Get the boys to help you. Joe and Davie are old enough to do chores when they get back from school.'

She was just as thrilled with the three large bedrooms and box room upstairs. Alfie had made beds for the boys and there was still room enough for them to play, and a large cupboard to hang their clothes.

'You can have the front room and I'll take the smaller one at the back.'

Was now the time to tell him she had changed her mind about sharing his bed? There was only one thing holding her back and this was the thought that being intimate with Dan might well get her in the family way. If Ada was anything to go by she could have half a dozen children round her skirts in as many years. No, she wasn't ready for that, so would leave things as they were for a while.

'I think the curtains from upstairs will do in the small bedroom and the box room. The parlour curtains might fit in the big bedroom but I'll have to make fresh ones for the front parlour and the other room downstairs.'

'Now I'm in business with Alfie, I can get the offcuts for next to nothing and good timber at half the price he has to pay. I'll have a bit extra each week for luxuries and such.'

They hurried round closing all the windows, making sure their new home was safe from vagrants. The sun was setting when they got back and the house was quiet.

'I think Betty has put the boys to bed – much earlier than usual, but I expect they were tired.' She found her brother and her friend in the backyard, and when Alfie got to his feet she hugged him. 'Thank you so much for your wedding gifts. I love my new house and the boys will too.'

'That's all right. It's the least I could do for me big sister. Your

Dan working at the timber yard has been a godsend. I reckon in a year or two I'll be able to afford a house like your new one in Greenstead Road.'

Sarah noticed that Betty couldn't hide her smile at his words. She obviously thought she would be with Alfie when he moved into the house he was hoping to buy.

2

By the time they'd walked up Hythe Hill, Alfie decided there wasn't much point in Betty coming round to his cottage in Maidenburgh Street.

'I'll walk you home, Betty. You don't want to be late.'

'There's no need, Alfie – I can walk myself. You obviously don't want me to come in so I'll leave you here.' With a toss of her head she marched off. He shrugged and let her go. She probably expected him to call her back or something, but he wasn't going to start those sorts of games.

Dan had said he better watch himself as Betty had her toe in the door already, what with all the pies, cakes and such she had been baking him these past few months.

'Come along, Buster, let's go home. I've got a busy day tomorrow if we're going to get that table finished for Mr Hatch by Monday.'

He strolled along the High Street and turned into East Stockwell Street, stopping to greet people he knew. The two boys he employed to push the carts would be waiting at the cottage. He trusted both of them. They were brothers and lived down the street from him. Their ma and pa were good folk but, like most around here, could do with a few extra pennies to make ends meet, and Dickie and Bill's earnings did just that.

As he didn't want them to go through the house he left the yard gate open for them. They were sitting on the back step waiting for him. 'Did you have a good day, lads? How much have you got for me?'

Dickie, at ten years of age and the oldest by a year, pointed to a pile of coppers. 'I reckon we did all right, Alfie. There's three shillings and sixpence and a few farthings as well. Mrs Kelly – she what lives round Queen Street – wants us to do a regular run for her to collect her groceries and suchlike.'

'Good boys. Take a tanner each – you've earned it today. See you Monday morning bright and early. You'll need to take the big barrow as there's the table to deliver.'

'Ta ever so, Alfie. We'll not be late. Did the wedding go all right?'

'It were a good do. My sister was that pleased with the furniture and the new house. If business carries on doing good, I reckon I'll be able to move nearer to the timber yard next year.'

Dickie nudged his brother – Bill weren't too clever, but he was a good worker and never complained.

'You would be nearer the yard, Alfie, but it would be a bugger to get the furniture to your customers this side of town. I reckon it's easier to push a barrow full of timber up that bleedin' hill than it would be delivering somethink what you've finished.'

'You might be right, but I'd like to be closer to my sister and get a bigger drum.'

'When you and Betty get wed and the monkeys start arriving...'

'That won't be happening, not for a long time anyway – maybe not at all. I ain't old enough for all that hogwash.'

The boys picked up their coins and dashed off. He was satisfied with half a crown for today's take as he hadn't had to lift a finger himself to get it. Dan buying his house made Alfie think it was time he did the same. He had a goodly sum lodged in the bank – his ill-gotten gains from his time as a thief in London – and what better way to use it than to buy the cottage he was living in. If he owned it then he wouldn't be beholden to Hatch. Next time he saw the bloke he would make him an offer for the cottage.

At dawn on the Sunday morning he was up with the lark and walking along the river with Buster. He loved this time of day, everywhere quiet, the air sweet-smelling. He blinked away unwanted tears as he recalled the untimely death of his best pal, Jim. He would have loved it here, away from the smog and smoke of London, but it weren't to be.

His friend weren't in a better place; he were just gone.

His dog was floundering around in the river, sending a flock of ducks quacking into the air.

'Out of there, you silly bleeder. You won't catch none of them, not in a month of Sundays.'

Buster heaved himself up the bank but knew better than to shake himself close to his master. The streets were empty at this time. This were the better part of town with decent folks observing the Sabbath and, unlike him, they would dress in their best and parade at church later on.

He made himself a pot of tea, fried up a bit of bacon and a couple of eggs from Sarah's chickens. His dog waited patiently in the yard for his breakfast. Alfie always cooked an extra slice or two of everything to give his dog. He reckoned Buster meant more to him than even his sister and certainly more than Betty. They'd been through a lot together and he didn't know what he'd do when the dog croaked – it would be as bad as losing Jim.

Still, no point in worrying as Buster was fit and healthy, and not even any white on his muzzle. He'd no idea exactly how old the dog was, but no more than five or six he reckoned.

* * *

He was just finishing the final polish on the table that had to be delivered the next day when his dog growled. The only person the animal didn't like was his landlord, and main customer, Mr Hatch.

'Settle down, Buster, he ain't going to do us no harm.' He weren't too keen on the bloke himself, but needs must, and he had no choice but to work for him until he had more customers of his own. Also, he wanted to buy the cottage and wouldn't be able to do that if his landlord took umbrage.

The man was smartly dressed, polished boots and a handsome gold pocket watch prominently displayed. He reckoned the bloke to be in his forties. He was what Betty called 'a fine figure of a man'.

'Good evening to you, Alfie. I've got a bit of business that you might be interested in.'

Alfie wiped his hands on the apron he'd taken to wearing when he was doing his carpentry. 'What's that then? I can't take on any more work – I'm booked up until next year.'

'No, nothing like that. Ain't you going to ask me in? I could do with a cuppa and what I have to say is better said indoors away from prying ears.'

'I ain't interested in anything illegal, so best keep that information to yourself. I make my living honest.'

'Fair enough. I could do with a man like you on my payroll, Alfie Nightingale. If ever you change your mind…'

'Thank you, but I doubt that I will. Come in anyway – I'll put the kettle on. There's something I want to ask you.'

When he put forward the suggestion that he buy the cottage, Hatch nodded. 'You got fifty pounds? It's yours if you have.'

'You get the deeds drawn up, I'll have a draft waiting for you soon as I've been to the bank.'

They parted on good terms and Alfie couldn't stop smiling. He'd gone up in the world and no mistake – a house owner at sixteen years of age was something to be proud of. Dan had had to take out a mortgage but he'd got all the money put by so wouldn't owe nothing to no one.

This suited him just fine – he were now in a better position to be able to turn down work from Hatch as he weren't in danger of being evicted. He would prefer to be out in the country like Sarah, but this cottage would do for a start. He was a legitimate businessman now and any money he made would be by honest work.

As he was sitting on the back step enjoying the last of the evening sunlight, his stomach clenched. Why had the man thought he might be a shyster like himself? Had the bastard somehow discovered his illegal past?

* * *

The children slept in the next morning, which gave Sarah time to get dressed in peace and prepare Dan and herself a tasty breakfast.

'That were grand, Sarah love, just what a fella needs on a Sunday morning. Are we going to matins as usual?'

'We were in church yesterday saying our vows, so I don't think it will matter if we miss today. We can go if the boys are ready in time, but I'm not going to wake them up. They need their sleep after all the excitement of yesterday.'

'We have to be out of here by the end of the month – that gives us ten days to move our stuff. I've got a couple of mates coming at the end of the week to take out the range and put the old one back, so you'll have to manage with that until we move.'

'It won't be for long, and I've managed on a lot less in the past.' The few months she'd spent living in a damp, dirty, mice-infested room in the worst part of Colchester was best forgotten. She thanked God she would never have to endure such circumstances again.

'Alfie's coming down with his two boys and his three barrows to give us a hand, but I don't know what day it will be. I reckon I'll be at work so you'll have to do it on your own.'

'I've got the boys to help me. Now John is four he doesn't need quite so much looking after, and Joe and Davie are a real help to me most days when they get back from school.'

He dropped his cutlery with a clatter and pushed his plate away. 'I'm hoping they'll stay at school until they're fourteen – there's nothing like a bit of learning to get you ahead in this world. Then they can join me at the yard.'

'I think Davie is keen to work with you but Joe wants to go to sea as a cabin boy. Robert Billings told him when he's ten or eleven he'll find him a position on whatever vessel he's sailing in.'

'Fair enough, I'll not stand in his way if he wants to be a sailor, but I don't want him to leave school so soon. There's still a bit of clearing up to do in the yard and the chickens want cleaning out. I'll get on with that; you have a bit of a sit-down, love.'

'No, both those are my tasks. It's you that should have a sit-down. You work too hard as it is.' She collected the dirty crockery and cutlery and took it into the scullery. The boys could have boiled eggs and soldiers when they eventually appeared. She also had a pot of jam to finish up before they moved, so they could have some of that on toast as well.

'The boys can do the chickens and tidy the yard. After all, it was the games they played that made the mess.'

He stood up. 'I reckon I'll go to the new house and paint the hallway then. Why don't you join me later? Bring a picnic lunch and we can sit in the garden to eat it. The boys will be made up to see where we're going to be living next week.'

He collected his tool bag and strode off. She could hear him whistling and her heart skipped a beat. When she'd first met him, when his wife Maria had been alive and she was their maid of all work, he had rarely smiled and she'd never heard him whistle at all.

He had loved his wife, but not in the same way he loved her. Dan was a good man and she had it in her power to make him even happier. She came to a decision. She would move into his bed at the end of the year – a kind of Christmas present for him.

* * *

The boys were eager to see their new abode and even the littlest didn't complain about the long walk from their cottage in The Hythe to the house in Greenstead Road.

'Quickly, across the road whilst it's clear. Joe, you and Davie will have to cross this twice a day when you go to school, and you must promise me you'll be vigilant.'

The boys nodded. 'It'll take us a good while to get there so we'll have to set off early. We'll get the strap if we're late,' said Joe.

'I'll make sure you're up in time, so don't worry, Joe. I expect some of the children have further to come and not all of them have stout boots and warm clothes in the winter either.'

There was no need for her to point out which house was going to be theirs, as Dan appeared at the front gate. The three boys took off, leaving her to walk more sedately the remaining hundred yards, carrying the heavy picnic basket on one arm.

When she reached the gate they had vanished inside and she could hear them running about, shrieking and exclaiming in delight at everything they saw. She was relieved to put down her burden on the table. Today they would be obliged to drink water with their sandwiches and cake, but coming from their own well it would be sweet and fresh and no danger to them.

She was sure a lot of ailments came from drinking dirty water – she remembered her ma had always told her to boil water before she gave it to Tommy. Her eyes filled as she recalled the dreadful day her little brother had drowned and her life had changed forever. It seemed a lifetime ago, yet it was only three years since the tragedy.

She wondered what her mother was doing now. Had she and her stepfather found employment wherever they went? Jack Rand had been a skilled tailor and Ma was just as good – hopefully they would have found employment somewhere else and were doing as well as she and Alfie were. She didn't blame her ma for leaving – she'd been a good mother to all of them – but that Jack Rand was a nasty bit of work and she'd have had to do whatever he told her to.

Dan and the children burst in. The boys were full of what they'd seen and how excited they were to be moving to their new home soon.

'It's going to be lovely, boys, so much more room and we will be able to grow all our own vegetables.'

'Pa says we can get a pig; I'd like a pig, Ma,' John said.

'We'll see. There's certainly room enough to build a sty at the bottom of the garden. We have to get settled in first before we add anything else to the household.'

'Pa says we can have a cat to keep down the rats and mice and maybe a little dog too,' Davie told her.

She smiled at Dan and he winked. 'Wash your hands, boys – we're going to eat our lunch now. I shall put the blanket on the grass. It's lovely and warm outside, even though it's the middle of October.'

The children were happy at the prospect of helping with the garden and wanted to start immediately. Fortunately, Dan had already accumulated a selection of tools – none of them new but all still serviceable.

Dan completed the decorating of the hallway, and she and the boys managed to weed one-third of the plot between them. Hot and dirty but content, they returned to their home at The Hythe.

'Play in the yard, boys, whilst I get us tea. We shall all have a bath tonight if the water in the copper is hot enough.'

She got the galvanised tin bath down from the scullery wall and put it in front of the range. This supplied sufficient hot water for washing the dishes and filling the kettle but not enough for the entire family to bathe.

Dan brought in the last two buckets and tipped them into the tin bath. 'There you are, love, that should be all right for the boys. I filled the copper again, so if you don't mind waiting until bedtime, it should be hot enough by then for us both to have at least a strip wash.'

'I'll have a bath even if the water's tepid. I don't want to go to my bed as I am.'

'Righto, you use the bath and I'll do my ablutions in the scullery when the boys are asleep.'

* * *

As always Dan remained in the yard whilst she was bathing, but she was aware that he would come to her side in a flash if she called his name. She might be an innocent, but she'd have to be blind not to see the way he looked at her.

It would be so much easier if she reacted in the same way to him. She loved him, loved his sons as if they were her own, but he didn't make her heart pound, or her palms tingle the way Betty said they should if she fancied a bit of how's your father.

Were her friend and her brother already doing it together? Surely not – Betty wouldn't risk getting into trouble and losing her excellent position looking after the children of Grey Friars House. Would Sarah rather be there doing the job she had loved before she had been dismissed, or was she happier being married to Dan and about to move in to the sort of house she had only dreamt about in the past?

She stood up and wrapped herself in the towel. It wasn't fair to her husband to stay in the altogether in the kitchen any longer than was strictly necessary; therefore she prepared to go upstairs to dry herself and get into her nightdress.

'Dan, I'm finished and the water's still warm enough for you if you want it.' Not waiting for him to reply, she scampered up the stairs and into the main bedchamber – the one that should rightly be occupied by both of them. He had given it to her several weeks before they were married and had moved up into the attic. He said it was so she could see to the children more easily, but she believed this was just putting her ahead of his own needs – something he always did.

She was the luckiest girl in the world and no mistake. She had a handsome, loving husband who was a good provider and an excellent father to his children. In a few days she would be living in a perfect home and it was high time she stopped being foolish and held up her side of the bargain.

When they were settled in Greenstead Road she would invite Dan to share her bed regardless of the fact that she might fall pregnant immediately.

* * *

Alfie sent Dickie and Bill out with the finished table and returned to his workshop to complete the finishing touches on a dresser. Making the furniture was the easy part – but it were bloody hard work sanding and polishing the finished articles.

The old codger from next door tottered out of the bog whilst still buttoning up his trousers. Alfie reckoned it was too dark in there, and smelt too rank, for him to do it inside.

'Morning, Alfie lad, you busy this morning?'

'Lots to do, Sid, but I ain't complaining. The more work the better. Do you need me for something?'

'There's a tile slipped. Thought you might be able to push it back from inside. I ain't able to stand on nothink meself, or I'd do it.'

'I'll come in after tea, if that's all right, but I've gotta get on now.'

The stench from the overfull privy made him gag. It were due to be emptied tonight. The gantway – the narrow alley that ran between his house and the backyard of the ones behind – was just wide enough for the night soil men to push their carts. They came once a week and it were best to keep the window shut that night. He was lucky he only had to share the bog and his yard with Sid and his missus. They were old folk, their children long gone, and he scarcely saw them.

When Betty came round she always cooked enough to take next door and he liked that in her. A lot of girls in her position, those what had a good job in a grand house, looked down on them not so fortunate. His girl, and he supposed he had to think of her as that, was as kind and generous as his sister and a pretty little thing as well. He could do a lot worse when it came to settling down – but he just weren't ready at the moment.

The boys picked up a couple of deliveries, but it had been a slow day – market day was best. Plenty of folk wanted their purchases taking home.

'The dresser can go tomorrow, lads, and then we need to go down the timber yard. We're going to move stuff for my sister first and then get the wood. Dan will have it stacked and ready in the usual place.'

He made do with bread and cheese for his tea and finished off the apple pie Betty had made a couple of days ago. It didn't take him long to push the tile back, and after he'd done it he wished his neighbours goodnight and set off for his nightly stroll along the river so Buster could relieve himself and chase a few rabbits.

Usually he was out until dark, but tonight his dog was ready to return much earlier. As he approached the side passage where the gate that led into his backyard was situated, Buster began to snarl. Something was up.

He put his hand on the dog's head. The noise stopped but the animal's hackles were stiff; the dog was ready to attack whoever was lurking in the yard. Unless Alfie left through the front door he couldn't bolt the yard gate, but as this were a decent neighbourhood he didn't bother when he was only going to be out for an hour.

Slowly he pushed the gate open with one hand whilst keeping the other on Buster. His neighbours were asleep – their house locked and silent. He moved stealthily towards his own back steps, knowing from the dog's reaction that whoever it was, was inside and not in his workshop.

There was the glimmer of a candle coming from a bedchamber. The bastard was upstairs going through his private papers.

'Go on, boy, you get him for me.'

The dog didn't need telling twice. He was through the door and up the stairs before Alfie had time to take more than two steps inside. There was a hideous scream and then the cottage fell silent.

3

Alfie pounded up the stairs expecting to find a mutilated body and his dog crouched over it. He burst into the back bedroom, the one he used as his office.

'Get this bleedin' dog of me, Alfie, before he rips me throat out.'

Spreadeagled on the boards was an old mate of his, Bert Sainty, a bloke who worked for Hatch.

'What are you doing in me house? I ain't getting Buster to go nowhere until you tell me.'

The dog continued to snarl and Alfie saw there were blood on his teeth. He had bitten the blighter already. He sniffed – there was a rank smell and it was coming from Bert. He'd crapped himself.

'Hatch sent me to have a squint at your stuff. I've not seen nothing up here and I'd not tell him if I had.'

'Why's your governor so interested in me? I ain't going to work for him, if that's what he thinks.'

'He asked about you and I told him what happened with your Tommy and that. He reckons you couldn't be so well set up if you hadn't been up to no good. I reckon he wants to know where you got the money to buy this place.'

'It ain't none of your business where I got my rhino from. Now, clear off and don't come in here again or I'll let my dog kill you.'

He snapped his fingers and Buster moved back a pace, allowing Bert to scramble to his feet and vanish down the stairs. The room reeked of shit and there was a nasty brown patch on the boards. 'Come along, Buster, we better lock up after that bastard and then I'll give the floor a good scrub.'

He didn't sleep much that night. He wasn't happy knowing Hatch wanted something on him. Next time he was down The Hythe he'd take a wander along the quay and see if Captain Bentley was still coming up the river in the *Merry Maid*. If he weren't, then he'd be safe enough. If he were then there was a chance Hatch could put two and two together. He'd given a false name, Bertie Smith, when he'd gone aboard the Thames barge, but that wouldn't be enough to protect him as Hatch knew he'd run away just after his brother had drowned.

Bentley had sold him to a lighterman and when Alfie had managed to escape he'd taken the bastard's dog along with him. If Hatch found out, then he'd be at the man's mercy and forced to work for him whether he wanted to or not, if he didn't want the bobbies knocking at his door.

He'd been not much more than a nipper then, twelve years of age, about to turn thirteen, and now he were a man, just sixteen, and a foot taller and weighed twice as much. Three years was a long time and he hoped Bentley had forgotten about him by now. He was pretty sure the blighter didn't come to Colchester any more, but it would be worth finding out for sure.

When he rose the next morning, he had come to a decision. He intended to complete the orders he'd taken for Hatch but not take more, however good the money offered. In future, he was going to find his own customers – now Dan was part of his business there should be some orders coming from his friends.

Despite having scrubbed the boards last night there was still a lingering smell upstairs but he didn't like to leave the window open, although no one was likely to climb into the cottage that way. From now on he was going to be more vigilant about locking up his premises when he went out. This meant he had to use the front door, but so be it – he didn't want anyone else in his house without permission.

Bert wouldn't forgive him for what happened last night – he'd have to watch out for that one. He wouldn't put it past him to get his mates together and set upon him. As long as he had Buster by his side he'd be safe enough.

When Dickie and Bill arrived, they took a small barrow each and he pushed the large one. He was relieved to be getting out of the area and to be spending the day at the other side of town helping Sarah to move.

'It's a grand day, Alfie, perfect for going to the river. Ma says we can stay out as long as we like today, make the most of the good weather before it gets cold.' Dickie grinned and his brother nodded.

'My Sarah will make us a fine picnic, so we won't go hungry.'

They trundled over the cobbles, through the High Street, down Queen Street and then it were easy-going as it were all downhill to Sarah's home.

Dan would be at work, but he and the lads could get on without him. His sister was just sending the two older boys off to school.

'I'm glad you're here early, Alfie. There's a lot to do. Can you start with the furniture in the parlour? I think you will get most of it on your three carts. What about the range – do you think you can manage it on your big barrow? It's very heavy.'

'I don't reckon so, Sarah – you'll need a donkey cart for that. We can take everything else. Show me what you want taken after the parlour stuff – then you can stop at the new house and let us get on with it.'

* * *

The third time that her brother and his boys arrived at the new house they were accompanied by Joe and Davie who had finished school for the day.

'See how much your Uncle Alfie has fetched today, boys. All we need now is the range to be brought here and fitted, and we can move in.'

John took his brothers around the house to show them what had been achieved. Most of the crockery and kitchen utensils were safely put away in the new dresser and cupboards. The beds were made, the clothes were in the closets and chests of drawers, the curtains were hung and it felt like home already.

Her brother unloaded the last of the items and mopped his brow. 'It ain't natural, being so hot at the end of October. Dan's mates are putting in the old range and they've got the bloke with a donkey and cart to bring it up to you. You don't need to go back to the old place – this is your home now.'

'I can't thank you enough, Alfie – you've given up a day's work for us. Let me give you something for the lads. I don't want them to be thinking they had to work for nothing.'

'Don't you worry about it, love. I'm not short of a coin or two and I'll see them right. We've got to get off now, get to Hawkins Yard and collect the timber your Dan has put by for us.'

'I shall walk back with you. Just give me a minute to collect the boys. I want to check there's nothing left behind. I can't believe you managed to catch the chickens and bring them here for us. I was worried somebody would steal them if they were there on their own.'

'I should stop where you are; let Dan check the house. No need to drag them boys away when they're enjoying themselves in the garden. You've done well for yourself. We both have, considering what we've been through these past few years.'

This seemed a good opportunity to question his intentions towards her friend. 'Betty seems to think you're getting serious – if that's not the case you should tell her. It isn't fair to lead her on.'

'If anyone's doing any leading on, it's her. I ain't thinking of getting wed for a year or two but if I do, it might well be to Betty.'

'Well just don't get her into trouble as you'd have to marry her then.'

'I ain't daft, Sarah. I'll not get caught like that, don't you worry. I'll come for a bit of lunch on Sunday, then, if that's all right with you?'

'We should be properly settled in by then. Thank you again for your help.'

* * *

Night had fallen before the new range was fitted and working. The boys had been happy with bread and jam for tea and had settled down in their new surroundings without a murmur of complaint. Her footsteps echoed on the uncarpeted boards upstairs as she made her way down to join Dan in the kitchen.

'They are fast asleep. I can hardly credit the move went so smoothly. It was thanks to Alfie and his boys. I'm going to have a cuppa before I go up and we can finish off the last bit of cake.'

'Nelly is going in to give the old place a good scrub. She's happy to carry on doing the heavy work for you even though it's a bit of a walk for her to come here.'

'It's going to be a trek for all of us, but it's worth it. The neighbours seem nice enough, Mrs Dodds next door says there's a carter we can use on market days to bring our purchases home. That will be a help as I didn't fancy walking the three miles with a heavy basket.'

'I'll kill a cock bird for Sunday, love, seeing as it will be our first one here. I thought you might like to ask Mr and Mrs Davies to come – make it a bit of a celebration.'

'I can ask them when I go past tomorrow on my way to the market. I hope John can manage the walk as he's not used to going so far.'

'I reckon you might be able to get a lift back with the carter. If he's bringing your vegetables and such I don't see why he couldn't put our little one on there somewhere.'

* * *

He went out to shut up the chickens for her while she washed up their mugs and left everything spotless for the morning. Every time she'd looked at him this evening there'd been a tightness in her bodice and a strange fluttery feeling inside of her. She'd made the big bed up with the best linen, put out her new nightgown, the one with a little bit of lace around the bodice and cuffs, but didn't know how to tell Dan that she'd changed her mind about consummating the union.

Her monthlies had just finished; she wouldn't have contemplated the notion of being intimate with him if that had still been going on. Her hair was freshly washed. She'd scrubbed herself from top to toe that morning, and she couldn't think of anything else that had to be done before she became his true wife.

What if he didn't want to do it? He'd told her he didn't want any more children, would rather do without having relations with her than risk her life in childbirth. It didn't matter – she was going to make the offer anyway. It didn't seem right not to after all he'd done for them. Most men would have taken what was theirs without asking but he wasn't like that – he was a kind and loving man.

She wasn't sure if she should say something to him before they went up, or leave it until they were both in their nightclothes. The boys' bedroom was at the back of the house. Whatever took place in the main bedroom couldn't be overheard and for that she was heartily thankful.

He told her not to wait for him so perhaps he was going to use the privy before he came in. She hovered nervously for a few minutes and then, when she heard him coming, lost her nerve and fled upstairs.

There was sufficient moonlight coming in through the window for her to see without the necessity of lighting a candle. This was fortunate as in her rush she'd forgotten to bring one. The sitting room curtains fitted perfectly and she pulled them closed just in case someone passing in the street below might see her as she undressed.

She was in her nightgown, her hair unbound and flowing around her shoulders, when she heard him on the stairs. Her heart was hammering so hard she didn't think she would be able to find the breath to speak.

The door had been left ajar and there was the flickering light of his candle approaching. If she didn't call out now he would be gone and she didn't think she'd have the courage to go and fetch him.

'Dan, will you come in for a moment?' Her voice sounded strange to her, as if it belonged to someone else.

Slowly he pushed open the door. 'What is it, love? Do you want me to light your candle?'

She couldn't speak. She nodded and he came in. From somewhere she found the courage to say what needed to be said.

'Why don't you close the door?'

Alfie was expecting to get another visit from Hatch but as the days passed and the man didn't come he thought the danger was over. When he'd been helping Sarah move he'd sent Dickie and Bill to ask after the *Merry Maid*; they'd gleaned the information that the barge no longer visited. Nobody knew why, but that didn't matter. As long as the bastard stayed away from Colchester that suited him.

Betty hadn't been round and he wasn't sure if that was because she had no free time or she was making a point. Either way, he was glad she didn't come and make eyes at him. There were a couple of girls down Barrack Street only too happy to give him what he wanted in exchange for a few pennies.

Sunday arrived and he secured the yard gate, made sure the back door was bolted as well as locked, and then went out via the front door. He was usually at home during the day so he didn't expect there to be any unwelcome visitors, but if any of Hatch's minions were keeping an eye on the place they would know he had gone out.

'Come along, Buster, we're going to visit Sarah and the boys. You can have a fine old time playing with them in the garden like what you did last time.'

The dog had a loop of rope around his neck at all times so

Alfie could grab it if need be. They were well known where he lived and children always ran up to pat the dog and offer him titbits.

When he walked past Grey Friars House he glanced up just in case Betty was at one of the windows, but they were blank. He strolled down East Hill, across the river and headed for Greenstead Road. It was like the countryside out here, the noise and bustle of the town gone, replaced by the sound of birdsong and the occasional shout of a child. There was little traffic on the street. Most folks would be at church or taking a well-earned rest inside.

He was still half a mile from Sarah's new home when he saw Joe and Davie racing towards him. He waved and gave Buster permission to join them. His nephews could talk of nothing else but how much they liked their new home.

'It's grand out here, boys, maybe one day I'll be able to come and join you, but I ain't got enough work to pay for such a smart house at the moment.'

'Pa's helping us dig the garden today. We're going to plant potatoes, carrots and cabbages in the spring and we might be getting a pig to fatten up as well.'

He ruffled their hair as they reached the front gate. 'Well, I might like to go in with that scheme; there's nothing I like better than a bit of ham.'

* * *

His sister were a good cook, even better than Betty, and put on a right good spread for lunch. He'd never seen her look so happy and Dan couldn't stop smiling.

He told them about the unwelcome visitor and what had happened, and they laughed. Whilst the boys and Sarah did the dishes he went into the garden with Dan to talk about the possibility of going shares in a pig. He also told him that he was now the owner of his cottage.

'I'll supply the timber to make the sty, go halves with the cost of the piglet, and pay for the butchery in return for a third of it. How does that sound?'

'Sounds fine to me – I've already spoken to the neighbours and they've agreed to save their peelings and such in return for a bit of bacon or ham when it's slaughtered.' Dan patted Alfie's arm. 'I didn't know you were a wealthy gent, able to buy your own house. I won't ask where you got the cash from. I wish I could have bought this outright, but as long as I keep up the payments it will be ours in ten years or so.'

'I didn't want to be beholden to that bastard Hatch – but I don't like not having much in the bank. It gave me a sense of security knowing I had money behind me – now I've got to rely on what I earn.'

'I give Sarah money for housekeeping and I know she puts a bit aside each week, as well as the money she gets from selling any spare eggs. I hope we never have to use it.'

'Being foreman at the timber yard is a good job. You earn decent money.'

Buster was racing around the plot chasing the boys and seeing them so happy made him smile. 'Joe said you're going to get them a puppy. If you're serious, I know for a fact that Buster's fathered a litter in Stockwell Street and they've got four puppies for sale. Shall I get one for the boys?'

'Go on then. I just hope it doesn't get as big as your dog. It will cost a fortune to feed.'

'No, you ain't got to worry about that, Dan. Buster catches rabbits for himself most mornings and I get an extra one every now and again for the pot.'

'Then bring a puppy with you when they're ready. I'll not tell the boys until you come. It can be your gift. I want a dog, not a bitch. I'll pay you for him.'

'You've spent a fair bit already on this move. Even though it didn't cost you for my labour, the new furniture still set you back. Don't get yourself into any more debt on Sarah's account, Dan; she'd not like that.'

His friend rubbed his eyes and smiled. 'Too late to worry about that. As long as I can pay off some each week, and don't add any more to it, she doesn't need to know how much I've spent or how much extra the mortgage is on this place.'

'As long as I can keep making furniture and you can keep supplying me with cheap timber both of us will prosper.'

He got back to his house as it was getting dark, and nothing untoward had taken place in his absence. Buster flopped down in his usual place on the kitchen floor and Alfie retired. His sister was happy. He reckoned she'd fallen for Dan after all, and he vowed that if anything ever happened to change that he would be there to support her. If it meant keeping Betty at bay, then so be it. Family came first as far as he were concerned.

4

DECEMBER 1845

'Just one more push, Mrs Cooper, and baby will be here,' Nurse Digby, the local midwife, said briskly.

Sarah didn't think she had the energy to push even once more – her labour had been long and painful and she was exhausted. From somewhere she summoned the energy and bore down with all the force she had.

'Here you are, a beautiful daughter, strong and healthy, just like I said she would be.' The infant's lusty cries filled the room and made up for everything that had gone before.

She held out her arms and the nurse handed her the squalling bundle that had been hastily wrapped in the waiting warm towel. A daughter – now her family was complete. She stroked the soft bloodstained head and watched with interest as the cord was cut and tied.

'You hold on to her, Mrs Cooper, and then give me one more push so I can deliver the afterbirth. Then I'll clean up baby first and after that do the same for you.'

Dan would want to know he had a daughter, a healthy one this time, not like the tragic little baby that had been the death of his first wife Maria two years ago. He would want to know that everything had gone smoothly and so would Alfie and Betty. They were waiting downstairs for news and might not have heard the baby cry.

'Nurse Digby, would you take my daughter down and show her to Mr Cooper before you do anything else? He and the boys will be anxious for news after so long.'

'Do you have a name for her? She's a pretty little thing – I think she looks like you already.'

'As it's only a week until Christmas I'm going to call her Mary.'

She was a bit uncomfortable underneath but apart from that was perfectly well. She could do with a bit of a sleep, but that would have to wait until she'd spoken to Dan and the boys. No doubt Alfie and Betty would expect to come up and congratulate her as well.

Her brother and friend had got wed in the summer because Betty was in the family way and their baby was expected in March sometime. Alfie seemed more resigned to his circumstances than happy, but he wouldn't let Betty down and would be a good husband and father. She was certain her friend had got into trouble deliberately, had been jealous that Sarah was so happy and expecting her first infant. She hoped this hurried marriage would work out – but without love on both sides she doubted it would be as happy a union as her own.

It didn't take long for the midwife to clean her up and help her into her fresh nightgown. 'There you are, Mrs Cooper, all clean and ready. Shall I let them in now?'

Mary had suckled for a bit and then fallen asleep exhausted by her arrival into this world. Sarah was reluctant to part with her baby so she was still holding her. The beautiful cradle Alfie had made was standing ready beside the bed.

By the time her family had visited she was worn out and Dan, bless him, took the boys downstairs for a belated breakfast. She had been in labour for more than thirty-six hours and the last few had been the hardest. If she had her way this would be her one and only baby but she could hardly ban her husband from her bed – especially as they both enjoyed what they did in it.

As long as she was feeding her daughter she shouldn't fall again – at least that's what the old wives said. This didn't explain why some women produced an infant every year, because they must have still had a baby at their breast when they started the next one.

* * *

Sarah was up and about the next day and Dan went off to work satisfied she was well enough to cope with the three boys. The weather had worsened and it looked like it might snow by Christmas Day.

'Here, Joe, put this potato in your pocket. It will keep you warm on the way to school. If you put it by the fire in the school-room it should still be hot enough to eat at midday. Davie already has his and is waiting for you outside.'

'Are you well enough to look after John and Mary, Ma? You don't look too clever this morning.'

She hugged him and pushed him gently towards the front door. 'I won't be doing much. Nelly comes in today to do the heavy work. Off you go, son, and be careful crossing the road. It's a mite slippy today.'

He grinned and clattered off down the flagstone passageway. With his mop of floppy black curls and bright blue eyes he was just like his pa, and had the same kind nature as Dan too. Davie looked more like his dead ma, brown hair and lighter blue eyes. They were both handsome boys and hard-working.

Dan was determined they would remain in school until they were old enough to work – thirteen or fourteen probably – which meant Joe had another four years at least to learn his letters and numbers. John would be starting at the school after Christmas and the little boy was desperate to join his brothers and not be obliged to stay home doing chores.

Mind you, the older ones had plenty to do when they got back. There were the chicken coops to clean out – the pig had been slaughtered last week ready for Christmas. They wouldn't get a piglet until next year so for the moment that was one task they didn't have to do.

Mary was feeding well and no trouble at all. Apart from the dirty rags that needed washing out she wouldn't know she'd had her. Nurse Digby had said it would take a week or two for her belly to go back to normal and that she mustn't worry about still looking as if she was carrying.

'John, are you going to help me with the bread?'

'Don't want to, don't like doing baby jobs,' he whined.

She was about to remonstrate with him, but reconsidered. He was probably feeling a bit jealous of the new arrival – after all, until yesterday he had been the baby of the family.

'In that case, you can clean out the grate in the parlour and lay the fire for tonight. Only big boys can do that.'

Immediately he scrambled to his feet and put aside his lead soldiers. 'I can do that for you, Ma, and I'll fetch in the coal and all. But I don't want to empty the po.'

'You don't have to do that, love; that's my job.'

* * *

And so the days passed. Christmas came and went and the baby thrived. John was happy to walk the couple of miles to his school in the company of his brothers. Life couldn't be better. Her only concern was that her brother seemed more morose each day and it was obvious his relationship with Betty was strained. When they came for lunch on Sundays he was fascinated by Mary and she hoped the arrival of his own baby would settle him.

'I hope we have a girl, Sarah. I reckon I'd like a daughter. Betty thinks she's having a boy – wants to call him Harry if we do.'

'As long as the baby's healthy, and Betty's well afterwards, it doesn't matter whether you have a son or daughter. She seems a bit quiet lately. Is something worrying her?'

'Money's a bit tight since I stopped taking orders from Hatch last summer. She thinks it don't matter who I work for as long as they pay out on time. If it weren't for the barrows I'd not be making enough to pay me way. There ain't enough carpentry work at my side of town. He's put a stop to any of his tenants getting furniture from me.'

* * *

'It's a good thing Dan is doing so well at work as there's been little money from your side of the business lately. It's a godsend having such a good-sized plot of land so we can grow our own vegetables, keep chickens and a pig.'

Alfie forced a smile. He knew that his brother-in-law was getting deeper and deeper into debt, and if he couldn't find a bit more carpentry work Sarah was in for a shock. She could lose the house and if that happened they'd get nowhere near as nice a home as the other one neither.

'I've been putting a few pennies by each week so if you need to borrow it, you only have to say.'

'No, Sarah love, you hang on to it. You never know when there's a rainy day coming.'

'Don't say that, not when I'm so happy. I couldn't have a better husband and having Mary, as well as my three boys, made things perfect.'

'Don't mind me, love – I'm happy for you.'

'I just wish you were happy too. I didn't love Dan, not really, when I married him; but that all changed and I don't know what I'd do without him.'

'It was my fault she got in the family way – I could have sent her packing but I was too weak. There ain't anything I can do about it, so I have to make the best of it. I don't love her – but she's a good wife and she has enough love for both of us.' He'd had enough of this topic. Just thinking about how he'd allowed himself to be trapped made his stomach churn.

'I wonder what Ma would say if she could see us now. She wasn't a bad sort, but that bastard Rand made her leave. I'll never part with the pocket watch that belonged to our pa. Do you still have the handkerchiefs she gave you?'

'I do; they'll not be used. I've never seen better stitching. I'm sure she will come back one day to find us.'

Betty came in. 'I think we'd better get off, Alfie. I don't want to be walking all the way in the dark like we did last week, not with me the size of an elephant already.'

'I'll get me coat, love, and say goodbye to the boys.' He didn't like being told what to do, but she was right – if she fell it might prove fatal to her or the baby.

When they were safely home, Buster flopped out in front of the range in the kitchen. She put her shawl, his muffler and coat on the pegs behind the door. He thought it was time for a talk.

'You sit down, Betty love, put your feet up and I'll make us both a nice cup of tea.'

For once she did as he suggested without argument and

settled herself comfortably in the rocking chair he had made her. Once she was comfortable he joined her.

'I'm not making enough money from me carpentry nowadays, Betty, and we've got to cut back or we'll have to sell the cottage.'

'I told you not to break off with Mr Hatch – you'll just have to go back to him. I can't be doing with the worry, not with a baby coming in a few weeks.'

'I'm not crawling back to that bastard. I'd rather starve...'

'It's not you would be starving, Alfie, it would be me and your son or daughter. We're not getting into debt like Sarah and Dan – she might be happy but I can see how worried he is. He should tell her how bad things have become. It's not fair keeping her in the dark.'

'Don't be bloody stupid, Betty, he could hardly tell her when the baby was due.' Sometimes his wife seemed like a stranger to him and there wasn't a day went past he didn't regret having being obliged to marry her.

She burst into noisy tears at his harsh words and he went to her side. 'Don't cry, love. I shouldn't have spoke to you like that. You're right – I've got to put me scruples to one side. If I ain't working, then it won't just be us who suffer. I need to be able to help my Sarah if Dan goes under.'

She sniffed loudly and blew her nose on a rag. 'You promise me you'll go back to Mr Hatch and say you'll work for him again?'

'I'll go and see him first thing. Now, what's for supper? I fancy a bit of toasted cheese.'

'You go and sit down, Alfie love. It's my job to take care of you inside the house.'

He took her chair whilst she waddled about the kitchen getting things ready. He wasn't looking forward to going cap in hand to that bastard, but she was right – he was a husband and soon to be a father. He had to do what was best for his family.

* * *

He trudged round to Hatch's house first thing. For a man supposedly well off he lived in a modest home, not much bigger than the one Alfie owned in Maidenburgh Street. He told his dog to wait outside. No point in upsetting the bastard when he wanted something from him. He should have left Buster behind, but Betty didn't like to have the animal under her feet when he was out. They didn't really get on – just tolerated each other really.

He explained why he'd come. Hatch smirked and Alfie wanted to smash his fist in his face but held on to his temper.

'I don't like to be gainsaid, Alfie lad. You can't expect to get the same terms you got before. Also, I expect you to do other work for me on occasion.'

'I'll do the occasional job outside my carpentry, but only if I get the same as I was before for my furniture. I also want paying for the extra work.' He fixed the man with his best stare. 'I ain't doing anything illegal like – just collecting money in arrears.'

The man's eyes narrowed and for a moment Alfie thought he would be sent packing. 'Very well – you drive a hard bargain. I like a man who can stand up for himself.' He picked up the notebook and handed it to Alfie. 'There's a list of items that need making – you can get on with them straightaway.'

Then he went to a safe at the back of the room, fiddled about with the lock, and took out a bag of coins. 'This will cover the cost of materials. You'll get the balance on each piece of furniture when you deliver it.'

This had gone far better than Alfie had expected. 'Righto, Mr Hatch, I'll go down with me boys to collect the timber this morning. I reckon I can have the first order ready by the end of the week.'

He dropped the bag of money into his pocket, was on the

point of leaving, when Hatch spoke again. 'I'll be in touch when I need you for anything else – and I expect you to bring that dog with you. He's part of the arrangement.'

'Thought he might be.'

Buster was waiting for him, his ears pricked and his lips curled back in a silent snarl. 'Come on, old fellow, let's get out of here. Don't want to work for him but we have no choice – neither of us.'

* * *

March 1846

'Quickly, boys, we're going to see your new cousin. Your Uncle Alfie and Auntie Betty have got a little boy – he was born late last night.' Sarah had already prepared what she needed for Mary – it just took much longer to chivvy her sons. By the time they had all got their coats, mufflers, boots and caps on, a further half an hour had passed.

Alfie seemed very relaxed for a young man who had just become a father for the first time. Dan had left for work before her brother had arrived with the good news, so he didn't know.

'We're ready at last. I'm so sorry to have kept you waiting. Betty will be wondering what's become of us.'

'The midwife said I had a couple of hours to fetch you. She wanted to get everything tidy and for Betty to have a bit of a rest.'

'What are you going to call him?'

'No idea. That's her department. As long as it's not Jack, Bert or Ben, I don't mind.'

Sarah already knew that Betty was going to call the baby Tommy but she would leave it to her friend to give Alfie the good news.

John trotted up with the family dog, Spot, on a piece of string. 'No, I told you we can't take him with us. There's not going to be much room with all of us there and the last thing they need is another dog cluttering up the place.'

Reluctantly he pushed the dog into the scullery and shut the door. They all knew better than to leave him roaming around the house where he would cause havoc by chewing anything he could get his teeth into. Fortunately, Spot had taken after the bitch and not Buster. He was still a big dog, but not quite so massive. He more than paid for his keep by catching rats and killing them and, as Alfie had promised, he brought back a rabbit from the fields most days and was happy to share it.

The weather was clement for the middle of March. There were daffodils showing their frilly yellow heads in her front garden and from the racket the sparrows were making they were already thinking about their first brood.

Without being asked her brother took the baby and snuggled her into his coat. He was going to make an excellent father and she prayed having a little one would bring him closer to his wife. Since he'd started back with Mr Hatch he'd not been like himself at all.

Whilst the boys ran ahead with Buster she walked more sedately beside her brother. 'Dan is that pleased he's getting quite a bit extra from the furniture making now. I didn't like to ask, but I'm sure he was struggling to pay the bills without the extra.'

'I didn't want to work for Hatch again, but I was struggling too. I'm making good money and when I've got a fair bit put by I'm going to sell up and move down here somewhere. Get away from him once and for all.'

'I don't blame you and I know Betty would like to be close by.' She paused, wondering if this was the time to mention her worries about his marriage. 'I know you don't feel the same about

Betty as she does about you, Alfie, but she's a good wife to you and could make you happy if you would allow her to.'

'It ain't her – I've got used to her now. It's something else what's worrying me but it ain't anything I can tell you about.' He changed the subject abruptly. 'Dan says he's found us a piglet and we can pick it up on Sunday.'

'He has indeed, and if it does as well as the last one we will all be happy. It's times like this I wish that Ma was here to share the good news. Do you think we will ever see her again?'

'Not as long as Rand is alive – he'll not let her come near us. I reckon she might come back to Colchester if anything happens to him.'

'She is a grandma twice over now and doesn't know it.'

They turned down Stockwell Street and made their way to Alfie's cottage. Outside there were a few neighbours discussing the new arrival. One of them, Mrs Sainty, had been their next-door neighbour when they had lived with Jack Rand. The old lady came over and greeted Sarah with a smile.

'My, I can't believe it's you, Sarah love. Look at you now! Here, Alfie lad, give us the baby.'

Sarah shook her head. Mrs Sainty was even more dishevelled than she used to be; now she was little better than a slattern and reeked of gin. Her brother handed Mary to her with a grimace.

'It's good to see you, Mrs Sainty, but I need to go in and see my nephew. Come along, boys, remember what I told you. You must sit quietly in the front parlour whilst I'm upstairs with Auntie Betty.' Sarah took her daughter back.

The front door was open and they all trooped in. The children settled themselves in front of the fire and she followed her brother up the narrow stairs, eager to see the new arrival.

The bedroom was warm, a fire lit in the grate in honour of the occasion. The room was pristine, a cradle by the marital bed, similar to the one she had at home, and her best friend was sitting up holding the infant proudly in her arms.

'Do you mind if I put Mary down in that for a minute so I can have a proper look at your son?'

'Go ahead. I won't be putting Tommy down until I have to.'

Alfie's face lit up. 'Thank you, Betty love. I didn't like to ask, but that's the name I wanted for our son.' He leant down and picked up the baby then handed him to Sarah. 'Here you are, son, meet your auntie.'

'He's beautiful, Betty, and a good size too. Did you have a bad time?'

'I don't want to hear no details. I'm off downstairs to keep an eye on the boys. I'll put the kettle on and give you a shout when the tea's brewed. I expect you'd like a bit of toast to go with it, wouldn't you, Betty love?'

'I would that. I'm starving hungry after all that hard work pushing out the baby.'

He stopped at the door and smiled, looking happier than he had for months. 'I want to call the next one Jimmy after me mate what died.'

They could hear him laughing as he banged about in the kitchen.

'Blooming cheek. I don't want another one for a year or two, not if I can help it.'

Sarah perched on the bed beside her friend, still holding the precious bundle. 'I don't want any more babies for a while either. Dan is being ever so good about that and he's not come near me since Mary was born.'

'It'll be grand having Mary and Tommy grow up together and both of them having three big boys to take care of them. My Alfie's going to be a good pa like your Dan. He's busier than ever, making good money each week and even putting a pound or two in the bank for a rainy day.'

'You're lucky that he was able to pay for your cottage outright. I don't like having such a large debt to pay off. If anything happened to Dan – well it doesn't bear thinking about.'

Mary began to grizzle. 'Here, give me Tommy whilst you feed your little one.'

* * *

After an hour or so the boys were getting restless. 'I have to go now, Betty, and you need your sleep. I don't suppose you'll want to walk all the way to Greenstead this Sunday, but hopefully you'll come the following one.'

'We'll be there – Alfie wouldn't miss it for the world. It's the highlight of his week, being with all of you in that lovely house of yours.' Betty lowered her voice so she couldn't be overheard downstairs. 'He's not happy here. He doesn't like working for Mr Hatch. I'm that worried he'll fall out with him and then we'll be in the same position we were a while back.'

'He's got the family to provide for now. He won't make any rash decisions. Take care, Betty love, and see you soon. I'll try and visit again in a few days if the weather holds.'

Before she left she hugged her brother and the baby in her arms protested at being squashed. 'Are you going out to wet the baby's head tonight?' she asked.

His smile slipped. 'I'm going out, but I don't think there'll be any drinking involved.'

5

COLCHESTER, JUNE 1846

The months passed and Alfie's legitimate business prospered. He now had sufficient custom to believe he could manage without being involved with Hatch. He'd never told Betty where the extra money had been coming from and he didn't intend to do so now.

His son was thriving, but he found the constant wailing and smell of shit that surrounded him off-putting and he avoided contact with both his wife and child. Why couldn't she make more of an effort like his sister did? His niece always smelled sweet and the house in Greenstead was a pleasure to be in.

'Come on, Buster, we've got a visit to make and I might well need you.' He didn't bother to say farewell to Betty; they rarely spoke nowadays. He had moved into the truckle bed in the spare room, leaving her and the baby to have the front room to themselves.

Hatch welcomed him with his usual oily charm. 'I didn't expect to see you today, Alfie lad, but you're always welcome.'

'I'm not your lad, Mr Hatch. Show me some respect if you don't mind.'

'No need to be sharp with me, Mr Nightingale. You only had to ask.'

'I've come to tell you I'm severing the connection between us from today. I won't be coming out to do any extra business and I don't need any more orders for furniture. I bid you good morning, Mr Hatch, and thank you for your support over the past year.' Alfie turned to go.

The man's expression changed from friendly to formidable. 'Not so fast, you little bastard. You think you can pick and choose what you do around here? I own these streets and you with them. You're my man now and don't think otherwise.'

'I ain't nobody's man, and certainly not yours. Find someone else to do your dirty work in future.'

Buster was on his feet in the doorway, his hackles up, ready to leap to his master's defence if asked.

'You won't always have that bleedin' dog with you. You'll get what's coming – you'd better be looking over your shoulder from now on.'

Alfie marched out unbothered by the man's vitriol. Hatch didn't own him and he was certain nobody in his street would do him harm – they knew better than to anger his dog. However, he wouldn't go into any dark corners in future and maybe it would be best not to go to an alehouse in this neighbourhood.

* * *

He was busy in the yard finishing a dresser when his dog stood up, wagging his tail. Robert Billings poked his head round the workshop door. They had become good friends over the past couple of years and Robert always called round to see him when he was on shore leave.

'Good to see you. How long have you got this time?'

'I'm changing ship so I've got two weeks before my next berth. I'll give you a hand if you like.'

An hour later the dresser was finished. In the old days Betty would have come out to speak to Robert, brought them both a cup of tea, but since she'd had the baby she scarcely seemed to notice him, or anyone else for that matter. The only time she perked up was when they went to visit Sarah of a Sunday. Then she made an effort, and both she and the baby were spruced up.

'You've not seen my sister's house in Greenstead, have you? I need to order some more timber, so why don't you walk down there with me now? We can cadge a bit of lunch from Sarah – we'll not get anything here.'

'That sounds fine to me. Is your Betty out of sorts today?'

'She's not been herself since we had little Tommy in March. I'm damned if I know what to do to cheer her up. She used to be an under nurse, loved children. I don't see why she should find looking after one infant such a chore.'

'I can't help you with that one, Alfie. What does Sarah say?'

'I ain't told her nothing, don't want to worry her, and Betty is her old self when we go down there of a weekend. I reckon it's being married to me she don't like, but there's nothing she can do about it. It was her choice – she made sure she got herself in the family way and that I'd have to marry her.'

The lads didn't come in for a sandwich or a bit of cake any more – in fact none of the neighbours came round for a visit neither. Robert was right – he'd better speak to Sarah and see if she could help her friend.

* * *

Sarah was in the garden pegging out washing when Spot started to bark and ran to the side gate wagging his plumy tail. Then Buster's nose appeared in the gap between the fence posts.

'I'm coming, Alfie. I'll let you in.' She draped the sheet over the line and wiped her hands on her apron before hurrying to let her brother in.

To her astonishment he wasn't alone. Robert Billings was with him – she could see the top of his head behind the gate and there was no one else she knew with that colour hair. What were the two of them doing here in the middle of the day?

'Come in. What a lovely surprise. Mary's asleep in her cradle under the apple tree. I've just got to finish putting out these sheets and then I'll make us all a nice cup of tea.'

Her brother hugged her and Robert doffed his cap. 'I'm hoping we can scrounge a bite to eat as well, Sarah love. I hope you don't mind us coming unannounced like, but I wanted to show me mate here your new house.'

'Why don't you take him to see the pig. There's a bucket of scraps waiting to be tipped into the trough, and you could see if there's any eggs. You can take them if you like. The neighbours have already had theirs for the week.'

They strolled off down to the end of the plot. She could hear them admiring her vegetables as they passed. She was proud of the beans, potatoes, carrots and swedes that she grew. She also had a fine rhubarb patch, blackcurrant and gooseberry bushes as well as two apple trees. But she was even more pleased with the flowers in the front garden. She had three rose bushes, a gift from Dan on her last birthday, and the border that ran around the front was full of colourful plants. Folk often stopped to admire the display when they walked past the front gate.

The baby should sleep for another hour and would then want feeding. Mary was eating bread and milk, and vegetables mashed up in the gravy from the meat, as well as still taking the breast.

Sarah had just started her monthlies, which was a relief, because she didn't want another baby next year if she could avoid it.

When her brother and his friend came back the kettle was singing on the range and she was halfway through making them a couple of ham sandwiches. 'Make sure you've got no mud on your boots. I've just scrubbed the kitchen floor this morning.'

They checked, and satisfied they wouldn't bring in any dirt, the two men took a seat at the central table. 'Tea will be a minute or two, and I've almost finished making lunch. I've still got some rhubarb pie in the pantry and I'll get you a slice of that as well.'

Halfway through her sandwich she heard her daughter crying and immediately rushed out to fetch her. 'Hush, little one, your ma is here.' The cries turned to chuckles when the baby was picked up. 'Your Uncle Alfie is here to see you and he's brought his friend Mr Billings. Aren't you a lucky little girl?'

She finished her lunch juggling the baby on her knee, thankful she wasn't that damp. Robert wandered off into the garden to smoke his pipe, leaving her alone with her brother. She took in his worried expression.

'Is something wrong at home, Alfie?'

'It's Betty. She's not been right since she had our Tommy. I know she seems fine when she comes down on Sunday, but the rest of the week she mopes around the house and I'm lucky to get a hot meal when I finish work in the evening.'

'You should have said.' She looked at the handsome kitchen clock in pride of place on the dresser. This too had been a gift from Dan, but on their anniversary, not for her birthday or for Christmas. He spent far too much on her, more than they could afford she was sure, but it wasn't her place to criticise.

'The boys don't get home until late today – they go to Dan and spend the afternoon helping him. I'll go and see her now as it won't matter if I'm not here when they get back as he will be with them.'

'I'd be that relieved if you would, Sarah love. I don't know what to say to her nowadays. She ain't the Betty I married last year – that's for sure.'

'I've just got to feed Mary and change her bottom and then I'll go.'

'I'll carry her as far as the timber yard – I've got to go in and order some more wood on the way past. I'm not working for Hatch any more – gave him his marching orders this morning.'

'I'm glad to hear that. He's a bad lot. No one has a good word to say about him.'

* * *

Instead of handing Mary to her when they reached Hawkins timber yard, he gave the baby to Robert.

'No, you don't want to be carrying a baby about – let me have her.'

'I'm happy to do it, Mrs Cooper. I've got plenty of experience remember. I've got half a dozen younger siblings at home.'

He insisted on walking all the way to Alfie's cottage. 'Thank you for your assistance. It was much appreciated.'

'What time are you returning, Mrs Cooper? I've nothing much to do today, so would be pleased to carry baby Mary home for you.'

'That won't be necessary. It's mostly downhill and much easier going home. And please, call me Sarah. I think of you as a friend.'

He smiled, nodded, and strode off. She was pleased Alfie had found himself such a good friend – Robert was a good few years older than her brother – but this didn't seem to make a difference.

After all, Alfie had done more already than most men did in their entire lives.

She tried the side gate, the one that led into the yard, and it opened easily. For some reason, she didn't think that Betty would let her in if she knocked at the front.

There was no washing hanging on the line, and the back door was firmly shut even though the weather was clement. Not bothering to knock – after all she was family – she pushed open the door. The rank smell of unwashed dishes, dirty laundry and poor housekeeping made her gag. She had smelt worse, but it wasn't right her brother should live in this foulness.

There was no sign of Betty or the baby – they must be upstairs even though it was well after midday. There was a stout wooden box in the yard, ideal to use as a temporary cradle. There was no way she was putting her precious baby down inside the house at the moment.

She found a sack in Alfie's workshop and tied it around her waist as an apron. 'You be a good girl out here, Mary love. Ma's going to be just inside tidying up for your Auntie Betty.'

There was a copper in the scullery and it hadn't been used for a while. She went back and forth to the yard with the bucket a dozen times in order to fill the cast-iron container. Once this was done she lit the fire underneath. The water should be hot enough to do the laundry by the time she'd finished cleaning the kitchen. There should be sufficient hot water in the range for her to wash up the crockery.

She made no effort to be quiet, and in fact banged about rather more than was necessary, in the hope that Betty would come down to investigate. It took her an hour of hard work to get the kitchen back to how it should be. She put the kettle on and cut some slices of stale bread to toast in front of the range.

It was worrying that she'd not heard the baby cry or any

sound from her friend. She called up the stairs when the tea was made. 'Betty love, are you coming down for something to eat or shall I bring it up?'

There was a faint mumble and the sound of someone moving. Then a haggard figure appeared at the top of the stairs still in her nightgown. 'Bring it up. I don't feel too good today.'

Sarah looked out of the kitchen window, now sparkling, and saw that her baby had fallen asleep. She should be safe enough out there for a bit. Although the kitchen had been in a parlous state, the pantry was reasonably well stocked so Alfie must be buying food on his way home from work.

She draped her skirts over her arm and in the other hand took the mug and plate with the toast. As she passed she glanced into the back bedroom, where Alfie was sleeping now, and this was as it should be. The bed made, the window clean, and everything put away tidily. Unfortunately, the same could not be said for Betty's domain.

Again she had to hold her breath against the smell as she stepped in. She'd gone up with the intention of being sympathetic, of persuading her friend into doing something for herself. Seeing the poor little baby lying in dirty clothes, stinking like a midden, was too much for her.

'God's sake, Betty, you can't let little Tommy lie in his dirt. Do you want him to die from your neglect?'

She shoved the plate and mug into Betty's hands and then snatched up the baby. 'I'm going to give him a bath. Find something clean to put on him. You eat that and come down so you can feed him.'

Tears trickled down her friend's face but she didn't reply. Sarah didn't have time to help Betty. The health of her nephew, Alfie's precious son, was paramount.

She snatched up a blanket from the other room, found a clean towel and one of Alfie's shirts and then dashed downstairs holding the ominously quiet baby in her arms. She prayed she wasn't too late with her intervention.

She put him down gently in front of the range while she got together what she needed to bathe him. When he was unswaddled and could wave his little arms and legs around he perked up a bit. He wasn't emaciated as she'd expected, but surprisingly plump.

'Here you go, little man, you will feel a lot better when you're clean and smelling sweet and fresh like you should be.' It took her so long to get him clean that Mary was beginning to grizzle outside in the yard.

Then she heard her daughter chuckling and Dickie poked his head in the door. 'Me brother's entertaining your little 'un, Mrs Cooper. Is there anything I can do to help?'

'There is indeed. If your brother can keep Mary happy for a while then I can finish here. Do you have any money from your day's work?'

'That we do, missus, five bob. It's been a good day.'

'Then can you go to the baker's and buy some fresh bread, meat pasties and a few buns if they have any left.'

The urchin dug into his waistcoat pocket and put a pile of mixed silver and copper on the table. Then he picked out what he thought would do for his purchases and, with a cheery grin, he vanished.

She wrapped Tommy in Alfie's shirt and then placed him in the middle of the towel so he could kick and entertain himself whilst she filled up the tin bath for his ma. It was Betty's turn to get clean; she hoped she could persuade her friend to come down.

There was no need to fetch her as she appeared at the bottom of the stairs. 'I'm not coping, Sarah. I just don't know what's got into me since I had the baby.'

'Never mind, you have made the effort to come down now. I'm going to draw the curtains and close the back door so you can have your bath in privacy. I'll wash your hair for you as well. I think we'd better do that first, don't you?'

Once Betty's hair was safely wrapped in another clean towel, Sarah thought it safe to leave her to wash herself whilst she gave the bedroom a good clean and found all the dirty laundry. She was shocked to find a pile of freshly laundered clouts for the baby's backside, half a dozen nightgowns and two clean shawls in a chest of drawers. There were also fresh undergarments, and a clean gown she could take down for Betty as well. Surely her brother hadn't been forced to do this himself? It wasn't a man's task.

* * *

Alfie approached his house with the usual lowering of spirits. He didn't reckon Sarah could have done much to improve matters, not in so short a time. He went in through the side gate and was astonished to see a load of clean linen, clothes and baby items flapping merrily on the lines.

Buster's water dish was freshly filled and there was a juicy bone set beside it. The back door was open and an appetising smell of freshly cooked something or other was wafting out. He bounded up the back steps and walked in.

'There you are, love. Sarah's just gone. We've got meat pasties, onion gravy and potatoes for tea and a nice plateful of buns for afters.'

He couldn't believe his eyes. His sister had worked a miracle and his wife was restored to him. Her hair was shining, and neatly coiled at the base of her head; she smelt as fresh as a daisy and was dressed in a pretty cotton gown. The kitchen was spotless and everywhere smelled clean.

'Where's Tommy?'

'Didn't you see him? He's out in the yard enjoying the fresh air for a bit. Sarah found a box that works a treat with a blanket in the bottom.'

For the first time in months he was glad to be home. 'I'll just nip out and see him, then I'll tidy myself up and I'll be ready for me tea.' He paused at the back door and smiled at her. 'You look a treat, Betty love, and I give you my word that I'll not let things get this bad again.'

When he arrived Buster was already standing guard, his huge head resting protectively on the edge of the box and his son was stretching out trying to touch his muzzle. 'Good boy, Buster, he'll not come to no harm with you there.'

Satisfied his boy was safe and happy, he joined Betty at the kitchen table for the first decent meal he'd had in months – apart from the Sunday lunch he had every week with his sister.

'Sarah's going to come every day for a bit to make sure I'm all right. Knowing I don't have to do this on my own makes me feel better about things. I know I've not been a good wife or mother, Alfie love, but things will be different now.'

'That's all right then. I reckon I'll make a cradle for outside – I'll do another one for Mary. It doesn't have to be as grand as the cradle inside, just somewhere clean and safe to put the babies when the weather's nice.'

He stood up to clear away the plates but she waved him back. 'I'll do it; you've done more than enough these past weeks. Without you doing the laundry and such, things would have been even worse. I'm right glad you told Sarah. I was too ashamed to let on I wasn't coping.'

When Robert knocked on the front door and asked if he

wanted to go out for a beer, Betty told him to go. 'I'm going to pop Tommy to bed now, then I'll have a tidy-up and go up myself. You go on and have a beer – you deserve it.'

'I've locked the back gate, and I'll leave Buster in the yard. I'll come in through the front. I'll only have a couple of pints – I've got to collect the timber I've ordered first thing.'

It didn't get dark until ten and he had no intention of staying out any later. They went to the Red Lion in the High Street. It were a bit pricey in there, but he liked the hustle and bustle caused by the coaches coming in and out at regular intervals.

After a couple hours he was ready to go home. 'I'll be off to my bed, Robert. Are you still coming to give me a hand with the timber tomorrow?'

'Got nothing else to do and a few extra bob always comes in handy.'

Robert had agreed to work with Alfie for the next two weeks, which would mean he'd get a lot more finished. His friend was a competent carpenter. He weren't as good as him mind, but good enough to cut the wood for him and do the sanding and suchlike.

Sarah had invited Robert to join them for Sunday lunch. He hoped Dan didn't take umbrage. He were sure he'd not be too happy if Betty asked a bloke to lunch without his permission. Still, Dan was an easy-going sort of cove, didn't have a temper like what he did.

6

Over the next few weeks Sarah continued to make the journey into Colchester every day to help Betty. By the end of the month she was sure her friend was on the mend and would be able to manage without her constant supervision.

When they were sitting down to Sunday lunch, John mentioned it would be his birthday the following week, the first of July.

'I'll be six years of age, and Davie will be nine and Joe will be ten in August. Can we have a party like what we did when I was four?'

'I don't see why not,' Dan replied. 'We've got ample room here for a get-together. It will mean a deal of extra work for you, Sarah love, what with the garden, the chickens and the baby to take care of.'

'I think it's a wonderful idea. We can ask Mr and Mrs Davies, and Ada can come down with her brood so our boys will have children to play games with.'

'If I come down the day before, bring Tommy and spend the

night, we can make everything fresh first thing. It will have to be the Sunday, won't it?' Betty asked.

'I don't mind when we have the party – a few days late makes no never mind to me,' John said.

'Then that's settled,' Dan said with a smile. 'How many kiddies has Ada got, do you know, Sarah love?'

'She has two grown-up sons, Robert, and another one who takes after his father, plus six little ones. The oldest is about a year or two older than you, Joe, and the youngest must be at the same age as you, John.'

'Can we play Shinny?' Davie asked eagerly.

'I reckon you could – all we need are a couple of sticks and a cork from a beer bottle. We've plenty of room out the back, but you must keep away from the vegetable patch.'

The children scrambled from their chairs as soon as they were given permission to get down and rushed into the garden saying they had to work out what was going to be played at the joint party. Alfie and Dan followed them out for a smoke, leaving her and Betty to take care of the dishes. Both babies were sleeping soundly in the front room. It had been too warm in the garden today.

'Are things better between you and Alfie, Betty? Has he moved back into your bed yet?'

'Not yet, but I told him I don't want another baby for a good while and the only way to be sure about that is if he keeps his trousers on.'

'I've not caught on, thank God, but I expect as soon as I stop feeding Mary I'll be in the family way again.'

'You've got plenty of room for half a dozen children of your own. I'm not complaining mind, I love my cottage, we've ample room with just the three of us and a nice big yard for Tommy to play in when he's bigger.'

'I was worried that Dan wouldn't be able to keep up the mortgage payments but he assured me I have nothing to worry about now. We've even got a few pounds in a savings account for a rainy day.'

'My Alfie's doing ever so well too. He's got more orders than he can deal with and if it hadn't been for Robert helping out, he'd not have got some of them done in time.'

'I must remember to add him to the invitation list just in case his boat docks in Harwich that weekend. He's first mate now on a ship that makes the run from Harwich to Rotterdam every few days. I'm surprised he's not spoken for – a handsome young man like that.'

There was enough growing in the vegetable patch to make a couple of pies to go with the cake and iced buns. They still had plenty of ham left for the sandwiches and she had made some elderflower cordial for the children to drink. Alfie said he would bring some beer when he came.

She had made the boys a new shirt each as her birthday gift. Dan had bought them two lead soldiers each to add to those they already had. She had already told her husband she didn't want a gift when her birthday came in October, as she had everything she needed already.

The day before the party Betty arrived with Tommy in her arms and she was accompanied by Buster. Alfie would find it strange without his dog at his side even for one night. She had no need to bring anything else with her, as she could borrow from Sarah what was needed for the baby and herself.

'Alfie's meeting Robert tonight and he's going to walk down with him, his ma and her children, tomorrow morning.'

'Dan will be home at six o'clock and he said he'll get the trestles put up and help the boys with the bunting. The three of them are busy doing a bit of weeding for me – they seem to enjoy working on the land.'

'Didn't you tell me when we were sharing a room at Grey Friars House that your ma's parents are tenant farmers in a village not far from Colchester?'

'I did. They didn't like Jack Rand so we didn't visit them. I don't think my ma got on with them either for some reason. I think their farm was called Hockley Farm and is somewhere near a hamlet called Great Bromley. Perhaps one day I'll be able to go and see them and introduce them to their great-grand-daughter.'

'Why don't you write them a letter? You never know – they might be pleased to hear from you now that you and Alfie have done so well for yourselves.'

'I might do that when I have a moment to myself. The dough's proving under the tea cloth over there. It should be ready to knock back and make into bread and buns.'

The boys were so excited it took far longer to get them settled that evening than it usually did. Both babies were good as gold, the house was quiet and everyone in bed by full dark. No point in wasting candles staying up when there was nothing else to do.

It seemed as if she had scarcely closed her eyes before she was awoken by a thunderous knocking on the front door.

* * *

'Well, that will do for today. I reckon it's time to get washed up and go for a pint of ale,' Alfie said as he hung up his work apron, cleaned his tools and stepped back to admire the finished table.

'I've learnt a lot working with you. If ever I get tired of being a sailor I reckon I'll become a carpenter,' Robert said as he brushed off the sawdust from his person.

Alfie looked around expecting to see his dog flopped out in the yard and then recalled the animal had chosen to go with Betty and the baby. This would be the first time they'd been separated and he hoped his beloved pet didn't change his mind and come looking for him during the night.

'Shall we go somewhere else tonight? I know a couple of beer-houses we won't get our throats cut and it won't cost us but a few pennies for a good evening,' Alfie suggested as he washed himself under the pump whilst Robert moved the handle up and down.

'Why not? No need to spend more than we have to, especially as you've got a family to provide for now.'

As Alfie locked the front door and dropped the key in his pocket, he wondered if Hatch was still having him watched. If so, they would know he was without his protector and might choose tonight to attack him. He shrugged this off; after all it were a good while since he'd had words with Hatch and nothing untoward had taken place in the meanwhile. Anyway, he might not have Buster, but he did have Robert at his side, and he was half a head taller than him and certainly a deal heavier.

He heard two church clocks strike nine. He hadn't realised it was so late. It would be dark in an hour and he didn't want to leave his house unattended then. 'I've changed me mind. Let's go somewhere we can get a pasty or two as I'm sharp-set and I'm sure you must be too.'

As his friend refused to be paid for his work, Alfie stood him his supper and his beer. After a convivial hour or so he thought it time to leave. The streets were still busy with folk going about their business even though it was full dark.

He bid goodnight to Robert and strode out towards his home. He was at his door when a ragged street urchin approached him.

'Mister, are you the cove wiv that 'uge bleedin' dog?'

'I am. What about it?'

'He's been a wandering around the streets and Mr Hatch 'as gorn to fetch 'is barker.'

Alfie didn't hesitate. He had to get to his dog before Hatch did, or the bastard would shoot him without a second thought. 'Take me there. There'll be a tanner in it for you if you get me there before Hatch.'

The ragamuffin, it were hard to tell if it were male or female, run off, his feet making no sound on the path. Alfie raced after him praying he'd get there in time. If anything happened to his dog he didn't know what he'd do. He was scarcely aware of his surroundings, so eager was he to reach Buster.

Then the child turned down a foul alleyway and vanished. Only then did Alfie become aware that he was in a dangerous neighbourhood. The stench made him catch his breath. This was a trap and he'd stepped right into it.

The street was deserted. Not even a group of slovenly women with snivelling brats hanging on to their skirts. His skin prickled and he clenched his fists. He needed to get out of here – fast – before he was murdered.

Here the houses were so close together it were impossible to see any landmarks and get his bearings. He closed his eyes for a second, trying to picture the route he'd been brought on. He reckoned he were no more than half a mile from safety, but he'd not make it in one piece.

Perhaps if he kept to the shadows he might escape, but he doubted it. There was no one here who would come to his aid if he yelled for help – he was on his own and no mistake. He needed to find himself a weapon of some sort before the attack came.

His eyes adjusted to the darkness. There were no street lamps in this part of town. The faint glimmer of moonlight filtered down between the roofs, allowing him to creep along without falling over his feet. He hesitated, his back pushed up against the slimy wall, desperately searching for a piece of wood, stone, anything with which to protect himself.

Then his clutching fingers felt a brick shift. He swallowed bile. He daren't risk turning away from the street so reached behind him and pulled with both hands. The piece of masonry dislodged and his breath hissed through his teeth. It was better than nothing and might save his life.

If he didn't get nearer to his own area he was done for. With the brick in his right hand he edged himself along the houses expecting at any moment to come face to face with blokes with murder on their mind. Round here life was cheap. Hatch would only have to give them a bob or two and they would happily beat him to death.

He froze. His heart was hammering so loudly it were difficult to hear anything else – but he was certain there was a whisper not far behind him. They were looking for him – must be puzzled as to where he had gone. He continued to sidle along the stinking alley and dodged across an intersection. He'd been certain he'd come down this filthy lane earlier. He increased his pace and now could hear running footsteps behind him.

He stepped out from the shadows and ran for his life. He could see gas lamps ahead of him – he was going to make it. Safety was no more than a few yards from him. Then there was a searing pain in the back of his head and he fell forward. He curled into a ball trying to protect his vital organs. Booted feet smashed into his back, head and shoulders and then his world went black.

* * *

Sarah was out of bed in a flash. Dan was just as quick. 'Go down and let whoever it is in, before they wake the children and the neighbours.'

She snatched up her shawl, didn't bother to find footwear, and raced after him. As she reached the top of the stairs Betty appeared.

'What's all that racket? Is there a fire?'

'I don't know – no fire, at least not here.'

'I'll get my clogs and shawl and come down. Why didn't Buster bark?'

Until that moment Sarah had forgotten Alfie's dog was here. Whoever was outside, it must be someone familiar. As she reached the entrance hall she saw Robert leaning against the wall, his hands and shirt front covered in blood.

Dan turned to her, his face white, his eyes stricken. 'It's Alfie, Sarah love. He's been attacked and Robert's come to fetch Betty back to take care of him.'

Her friend hurtled down the stairs and arrived in a rush. 'My Alfie? Don't tell me he's dead.' She clutched her throat and swayed.

'No, Mrs Nightingale, he's alive all right – but he's been badly beaten. I left him with the doctor but he needs you at his side.'

Betty gawped at him. 'I don't know... I can't... What about little Tommy?'

'Don't worry, I can take care of Alfie. Can you look after the children here?' she asked Betty. Sarah didn't stop to ask Dan's permission. If her brother needed her and his wife wasn't up to the task, then there was no one else.

'I can do that,' Betty said. 'I'm sorry but...'

Dan took Robert's arm and led him into the kitchen. 'Go and get dressed, Sarah love. I'll put the kettle on whilst Robert has a bit of a clean-up.'

'Come upstairs with me, Betty. There's no point in everyone being awake. Mary sleeps until six o'clock and has bread and milk for breakfast. You don't need telling how to look after the boys – that was your job at Grey Friars House.'

'What about the party? The boys will be that disappointed.'

'It can go ahead without me and Alfie there – there's only the sandwiches to make, and Joe and Davie can help you with that and everything else. Dan and Robert will be here, and Ada will lend a hand too.'

When she got downstairs Robert and Dan were drinking tea and her husband handed her a mug. 'Drink this, love, before you go. Take Buster with you – Alfie will want him there.'

She was about to protest that she needed to get away immediately, but if Alfie's friend wasn't bothered about leaving then maybe things weren't as bad as she feared.

'What happened?'

When he had finished explaining she was shocked to the core. 'Why hasn't Alfie called the constable? Surely he isn't going to let Hatch get away with it?'

'He's got no proof it was that bastard behind it. You'll never find the street urchin who enticed him into danger. The constable will think he should have known better than to venture into such a place at night. Thank God I decided to follow him when I saw him go with that child. I arrived just in time to prevent them from finishing the job. Several of his neighbours came with me and we carried him back to his cottage.'

'Was he conscious? Has he got a lot of bones broken?'

'I'm not sure about the extent of his injuries, but certainly he's got broken ribs and he's cut and bruised.' He paused and his expression was grim. 'It's his hand. I reckon those bastards stamped on it. It's badly broken.'

She knew what this meant; her brother wouldn't be able to work at his chosen profession until the bones healed.

Robert drained his mug. 'He'll need nursing for a few days, but I'm pretty sure his injuries are not going to prove fatal.'

Sarah leant across the table and took Dan's hand. 'I wouldn't go, love, if I thought Betty could do it. I think she'll manage all right here even with two babies to look after. I told her the party must go ahead as planned – I'm sure the boys will understand why their uncle and ma can't be there.'

'Of course they will. Now, you get off and take care of your brother. Robert here says he'll be coming with his ma and the children this afternoon and can give me news of how things are going then.'

* * *

Buster seemed to sense there was something wrong as he kept growling deep in his throat and pressing himself against her as if she needed his protection. Robert escorted her to the door but didn't come in.

'I'll be getting home for a bit of shut-eye, Sarah, but I'll be around before I leave for the party.'

He strode off; her brother owed his life to this man. She would be eternally grateful to him – that's for sure.

The oil lamps were blazing in the front parlour and she could hear voices upstairs. The dog had already pushed past and galloped up to see his master. She gathered up her skirts and followed him. The young man in rolled-up shirtsleeves must be the physician. He nodded and smiled encouragingly. She didn't dare look at her brother who was stretched out on the bed with his dog beside him.

'Good morning, Mrs Cooper. As you can see my work is done

here. Mr Nightingale has been stitched up where necessary. His ribs have been strapped and his broken hand splinted.'

She forced herself to turn to her brother and couldn't stop her hands going to her mouth. He looked half-dead, both eyes swollen, bloody and half-closed, a row of stitches running from one side of his forehead to the other. His hair was caked with blood and there wasn't an inch of him she could see which wasn't damaged in some way.

'Alfie, what have they done to you? I can't believe you're still alive.'

'Neither can I. If it hadn't been for Robert I'd have kicked the bucket.' He winced and his voice trailed away, then he rallied and continued. 'Don't cry. It could be worse. It'll be a few weeks before I'm fully fit, but I've got enough put by to see us through this bad patch.'

His speech was somewhat distorted as his lips were swollen, but she understood him well enough. She scrubbed her eyes dry with her sleeve and managed a watery smile. 'I'll tidy up here, and make you a nice cup of tea.' She glanced at the doctor. 'Is it all right for him to have a drink if he wants it?'

The doctor nodded as he shrugged into his dark frock coat and collected his bag. 'The more he drinks the better. He needs to replace the blood he's lost as soon as possible. I'll be back later today to see how he goes.'

Alfie appeared to have dozed off, which was probably fortuitous. If he was asleep he would be healing and not suffering as much.

Once they were downstairs she was able to ask the question that had been foremost in her mind when she had learnt that her brother's hand had been broken. 'How long will it be before he can hold his tools again? He's a carpenter; he needs to be able to work.'

'Several bones were broken. His hand was stamped on. However, with luck he should gain full use of it in a month or two. If he tries to use it too soon it could be catastrophic. Keep him in bed as long as possible, Mrs Cooper. The more he rests the quicker he will heal. He's going to look worse before he looks better. The bruising will come out over the next few days.'

She dipped into her skirt pocket where she kept her cloth purse. 'How much do we owe you for your services?'

'There's no need to worry about that now, madam. I'll present my bill when my work is done. I'm just glad I was returning from another visit when Mr Nightingale was found.'

He departed and she realised she still didn't know his name. When she had lived in East Stockwell Street a few years ago there had been no doctor to call on. Everything was changing and not all of it was for the better. Mr Hatch hadn't got a hold on the area then, but now his pernicious influence had almost caused the death of her beloved brother.

* * *

The next few days were best forgotten. There wasn't a part of his body that didn't hurt especially when he moved. He was determined to get on his feet as soon as possible and start plotting his revenge against Hatch.

Dickie and Bill did extra shifts with the carts – even taking out the large one on market day. Robert called in every morning to take Buster for a walk along the river and Sarah took care of everything else.

Although he'd told his sister he could manage without the money he made from his carpentry, this wasn't strictly true. He'd already paid for the timber and if he couldn't complete the items then he wouldn't get paid.

The doctor's bill would likely take up half the money, and if he couldn't get off his arse and start working in the next few days he was going to lose everything. Betty had come home and to see her now you'd never have known she'd had any problems dealing with the baby. For some reason she quite liked the fact that he was unable to work and fussed around him so much he was ready to scream.

A week after the beating the stitches were removed. Most of the swelling had gone down on his face, and he could open his eyes properly. The bruises had turned from black, to purple and yellow but they no longer hurt. However, his ribs would take longer to heal and his bloody hand even longer.

Two weeks after his accident he felt well enough to walk down for Sunday lunch at Greenstead. He'd not seen Robert for a few days as his friend had gone to sea again and wouldn't have any shore leave for a few weeks.

He was determined to speak to Dan in private and the only way he could do that was if he forced himself to make the walk to his sister's house. They were having a cold collation today – it was too hot for a Sunday roast. Dan had set up a long trestle in the garden, the boys had carried out the chairs, and Betty and Sarah had put on cloths and such to make it look attractive. There were even a couple of pots with marigolds and daisies on the makeshift table.

'How's our pig getting on, Dan? If the ham from it is as good as what we ate for lunch, I'll be satisfied.'

'Come down and see him for yourself, Alfie. We can leave the womenfolk to their chatter and the children to their play.'

As soon as they were out of earshot Alfie broached the subject he'd been dreading all week. 'I don't like to ask, but I'm that desperate, I don't have a choice. It's going to be another few weeks before I can work again and I'm not making enough from the barrows to make ends meet. I'm hoping you can let me borrow something – I'll pay you back as soon as I'm on me feet again.'

Dan's mouth thinned and for a horrible moment Alfie thought his request was going to be refused. 'Without the extra from your furniture, I'm struggling myself. But I'll see what I can do. Maybe I can get a bit more against the house and we could split it.'

'That would be grand. I'll pay my half as soon as I'm working.'

Dan gripped his arm. 'Betty and Sarah don't need to know about this. We'll keep it between ourselves.'

7

Three weeks passed before Alfie was able to walk outside without heads turning to stare at him. He and Dan were thick as thieves but when Sarah questioned her husband he told her it was nothing for her to fret about – just man's business.

One Sunday they had finished lunch and were sitting in the garden. Mary was crawling now and had to be watched every second as she wanted to follow the boys.

'Tommy is thriving, Betty, and you look well too. I wish I could say the same about Alfie. Is he still not able to use his hand?'

'No, he can't hold a tool properly. He's going out with the cart but that can't be bringing in enough to keep us out of debt. He says we've still got a bit left in the bank and by the time that is gone he will be able to work at his carpentry again.'

'Dan looks worried – he's always smiling when he knows I've got my eye on him, but I see him through the kitchen window, when he's in the garden, and he doesn't look happy. We should never have moved here and taken on so much debt.'

'Have you spoken to him about it?'

'He just tells me not to worry – that he wants only the best for me and the family and he's not going back to a rented property in a rough part of town again.'

'At least Alfie owns our cottage outright. No one can take our home away from us.'

Their chat was interrupted by Buster and Spot deciding to chase the neighbour's cat up a tree. Both babies screamed, the boys added to the cacophony with their shouts of encouragement, and Dan and Alfie had to step in and sort things out.

As her brother and his family were leaving she found a moment to speak to him alone. 'When did the doctor say you could remove the splint?'

'He said leave it for a month and it will have been that long at the end of next week.' He flexed the fingers of his broken hand and winced. 'It's healing but it ain't right yet. I'm hoping I'll be able to hold me tools all right even if it's not perfect.'

'It's a good thing you had put by a fair amount in the bank. We're all missing the extra money and will be glad when things go back to normal.'

She hugged him and then kissed Betty and the baby. Buster shoved his huge head into her hip, demanding he get some affection as well.

'Get on with you, you silly great dog. See you next week.'

Whilst Dan was outside shutting up the chickens for her, and giving the pig the vegetable peelings, she checked the boys were asleep and that Mary had settled. The baby was teething and sometimes woke up grizzly during the night.

As always they sat together at the kitchen table having a last cup of tea and a bite to eat before they retired. 'I love Sundays, Dan – having all my family around me. I forgot to tell you that I got a letter back from my grandmother yesterday. She says she and my grandfather will call in to see us next time they are in Colchester.'

He looked up with a smile. 'I didn't know you'd written to them. They must be old folks now. I expect you miss your ma. Do you think they have heard from her?'

'They didn't say so in the letter. To be honest, I'm surprised they're still farming. I assume they are tenant farmers so I suppose if they leave they'll be without a home. I haven't any uncles or aunts so they have no one to help them.'

'Maybe Joe can get some work with them in a year or two? He's a big lad already, and loves nothing better than to be outside working the land and tending to the pig and the chickens. I reckon he'd make a good farm labourer. He seems to have forgotten about going to sea.'

'When they come, they can see for themselves what a help he could be. I don't know anything about their circumstances apart from what my ma told me and that wasn't much. She married my pa against their wishes and they didn't speak again – they didn't even come to Tommy's funeral.'

'In which case, Sarah love, I'm surprised they answered your letter. Anyway, I'm going up now. I've got an early start tomorrow as there's a load of timber coming into the docks and I need to supervise the unloading.'

She turned down the wick in the oil lamp that stood in the centre of the table and followed him. He carried the single candle. There was no need to take two up with them. The baby was sleeping peacefully in her cradle under the window, the boys were quiet, and she slipped into bed satisfied she would have a peaceful night.

When Dan reached out for her she went willingly into his arms. If she caught on now it wouldn't be so bad as Mary was already nine months old. She didn't think that Alfie and Betty were doing it yet. This was probably because Betty had managed so badly when little Tommy had been born.

* * *

Towards the end of September, they had finished Sunday lunch and were sitting in the garden enjoying the autumn sunshine. Mary was able to stand now and was determined to toddle after her brothers if allowed.

'Tommy is a healthy baby, Betty, and you are fully recovered. I wish I could say the same about Alfie. Are you and he not getting on?'

'He's still sleeping in the other room, if that's what you mean. I don't mind. I don't want another baby if I'm going to feel so poorly when it's born.'

'Now Mary's weaned I'll be expecting again soon. Is Alfie able to do his carpentry? His hand looks as good as new.'

* * *

Whilst Betty was in the privy Sarah followed her brother into the front garden. 'Betty says your hand doesn't work properly. What does the doctor say?'

'I've not seen him. I can't afford such luxuries. It's healed but it ain't right. I'm learning meself to use my left hand instead of this one but it's taking longer than I thought.'

When Alfie and Betty prepared to leave she embraced her friend and her brother and kissed little Tommy. 'See you next week,' she said to them all.

Later, as she and Dan drank their last cup of tea she smiled at him. 'It's the first day back to school for the boys and I want to make sure I have everything ready for them, but I won't be long.'

'Then I'll wait for you, love. I don't like going up my own.'

Sarah hugged him and he smiled lovingly at her.

It didn't take her long to collect the boys' freshly ironed

clothes ready for tomorrow. The boys were sleeping when she went in with their garments.

The next morning Sarah woke when Dan got out of bed, but he shook his head. 'You stay where you are, Sarah love, no need for both of us to be up so early. Wait until the baby cries.'

'I don't like to think of you going off without something hot inside you or having something to eat at midday.'

'I'll do fine, don't you fret, sweetheart. I don't know when I'll be back. Keep my supper warm on the range if I'm not here in time to eat with you.'

She was drifting off to sleep when she heard the front door open and close quietly. He was a good man. She'd never find better, and she was the luckiest woman in Colchester to have such a husband.

The boys woke her up with their chatter and she quickly completed her ablutions, dressed and washed and changed the baby, before rushing downstairs to put the kettle on.

'Come on, Spot, you must be bursting. We'll go and let the chickens and the pig out whilst the water boils.' With Mary on her hip and the dog at her side she hurried down the garden. Their approach was heard by the fowl and the pig. The children had christened the unfortunate beast Ham, which she thought was rather unkind in the circumstances.

She went into the shed that contained the grain and took a scoop before letting the birds out. They had plenty of water to go with the corn and she threw in some vegetables that had run to seed as well. There was still a pail of slops left from yesterday for Ham.

Once these tasks were done she opened the back gate that led out into the fields so the dog could go hunting for his breakfast. Rarely a morning went by without the dog returning with a plump rabbit.

Joe was chivvying his brothers into laying the table whilst he, his hand wrapped in a cloth, carefully tipped the boiling water into the teapot.

'Well done, boys – what a help you are.' She deposited her daughter in the specially built chair that Alfie had made. When this was pushed up against the table edge the baby couldn't fall out. 'Give your sister a crust, Davie; there's a good lad.'

By the time the children had finished their breakfast of boiled eggs and toast, she had made three sandwiches and wrapped each individually in greaseproof paper.

'Take care on the way to school, boys, and don't go near the timber yard on the way home. It's dangerous there when there's wood being unloaded from the river.'

'We won't, we promise,' they chorused and they burst out into the front garden and away down the path, laughing and shoving each other. They were fortunate that the teacher they had was a well-educated man who didn't believe in the overuse of the strap. Alfie had never been happy to go back to his lessons when harvest was done, but his nephews were different.

Nelly came in to do the heavy cleaning and laundry today whilst she got on with things in the garden. She had still to lift the last crop of potatoes, carrots and swedes and store them in the root cellar under the house. The onions were already harvested and had been plaited together and were hanging in golden strings in the scullery. There should be sufficient to last them the winter.

The soft fruit had been made into conserve and there were just apples to pick and store and then the plot could be made ready for winter.

It had been a glorious summer, apart from what had happened to Alfie, and she couldn't remember being happier. It might take a bit longer for him to be able to build his furniture the way he used to, but she was certain he would be making good money again before the end of the year.

Whilst her baby played contentedly with saucepans and a wooden spoon, Sarah decided to reply to her grandmother's letter. She had always had a neat hand and enjoyed being able to use it. She kept the note brief. There was little fresh news to give them after all, just said she was looking forward to meeting them after so many years and that they would be very welcome to stay overnight if that would be more convenient. Greenstead was on the right side of town for visitors coming from Great Bromley. Probably no more than seven or eight miles, a morning's walk, but too far for her to go carrying a baby.

She had just put Mary down for an afternoon nap when she heard the sound of heavy boots on the front path. Alfie had come to see her – an unexpected visit, but a pleasure nonetheless.

* * *

Alfie needed to earn a lot more than he was getting from the three carts. Dan had been left with the extra payments to the bank for the loan and, if things didn't pick up a bit soon, he was going to apply for a mortgage on his cottage.

He could hear Betty singing in the kitchen and this lifted his spirits a little. It wasn't her fault she had been poorly after the baby, but he was right glad she was back to her usual self now. But he weren't going to move back in the marital bed for another few months to give her a chance to enjoy being a ma.

'Betty love, I'm going down the timber yard. Dan said there's always wood what's damaged going for free. I'm not going to miss the chance of getting that. The lads have got half a dozen deliveries to do so won't be back until teatime. You going to be all right on your own?'

She appeared on the back step, her hands floury. 'You go off. I'm making us a nice steak pie for tea and some scones are going on the griddle later.'

'Righto. I'm taking the big barrow and I got a few coppers to buy meself something to eat at midday.'

Although he couldn't make something as complicated as a dresser or a chair any more, he could now knock up a simple bench, a bed or a side table, mainly using his left hand as he'd told Sarah the day before. He was going to make a few of those baby chairs he'd made for Mary and Tommy – he reckoned there might be a market for some of those.

It was easier going to The Hythe as there were only the one hill to push up, the one from his street to the High Street. Then it were all downhill – pity it weren't the other way round because it were a bugger getting the big cart home when it were full of timber.

His ribs had healed and he reckoned he were as fit as he'd ever been apart from the fingers on his right hand not working proper. He was tempted to sit on the cart and let it roll him down on Hythe Hill but thought better of it. He didn't want another accident.

Dan had said the best pickings would be along the wharf. Alfie reckoned he wouldn't be the only one on the scrounge. Folk around here were all but destitute; anything free was a godsend.

Buster stuck close to him. He didn't like the shouting, shoving and chaos that reigned alongside the ships. The delivery to Hawkins timber yard would arrive on a couple of Thames barges. Even the sight of the red sails made his stomach churn.

The boats had arrived with the incoming tide. It would be nigh impossible to unload anything when it were out as there were only mud, and the boats, barges and ships would be below the edge of the wharf. Although high water wasn't until midday there were dozens of dock labourers swarming over the barges. These casual labourers were lucky to get two and sixpence a day for working like slaves.

He reckoned his friend had had to be there at dawn to clear the yard for the new timber. He left Buster to guard the cart and started to shoulder his way through the press of folk. He expected there to be the sound of work going on by the ship, shouting and the clatter of timber being moved. It didn't seem right somehow – a bit too quiet like.

Something was up. 'What's going on, mate?' Alfie asked the cove standing in front of him.

'Some poor bugger's under that lot. The rope broke when they were hoisting it off the barge.'

Alfie pushed his way forward until he was standing in front of a massive pile of timber, half on and half off the barge. Men were frantically lifting planks, shouting to each other – or perhaps they were shouting to the man trapped underneath.

He moved forward intending to give them a hand but a smart gent in top hat and tailcoat waved him back. 'Stay where you are. We have enough labour to do the job.'

He glanced downriver and saw the tide had just turned and there were several bits of timber floating seawards. He pushed back through the crowd of gawpers and made his way to his cart. 'Come along, Buster, we've got work to do. Whilst the folks are watching them find the poor blighter what's been crushed, we can fill the cart.'

The barrow ran easily along the quay and he kept his eye on his prize. It wouldn't do to set it out in front of everyone – but if he were lucky and nimble he'd collect enough wood out of the river to make half a dozen items. It shouldn't take too much drying out. Brackish water would ruin the planks if they were submerged for long.

Once he was safe from observation he sat down and removed his boots, rolled up his trouser legs and shirtsleeves, and he was ready to make a grab for his prize as it drifted past. By the time he'd got a cartful he was soaked to the waist but that made no never mind. Free timber would be a godsend in the next week or two. With luck he could avoid having a debt on his own cottage and even start paying Dan back for the loan.

The crowd had thickened when he crept past at the back with his ill-gotten gains. If he hadn't been sobbled, his trousers soaked and clinging to him, he would have stopped himself to see how things turned out. What was an ill wind for somebody else had turned out to be a good day for him and Dan.

It took him two hours to get his bounty home. He carefully stood the heavy planks against the wall in the yard so they could get the sun on them. He'd expected Betty to come out – he'd made enough racket after all.

The boys weren't back from work yet so he couldn't lock the yard gate. He removed his boots and left them on the doorstep and then stepped into the kitchen dripping river water onto the freshly scrubbed boards.

'Betty love, I'm back. You upstairs?'

There was no answer. She must have nipped out for some necessities. He stripped off his sodden garments and draped them over the wooden rack he'd made to stand beside the fire to dry little Tommy's clothes when it was too wet or cold to put them out.

Whilst he was naked he thought he might as well give himself a wash. He didn't often get the chance to complete his ablutions with any degree of privacy. He dashed upstairs and found himself clean underwear, shirt and trousers and were just putting on the kettle when Betty and the two lads came home.

* * *

Sarah hurried to the front door and opened it. Her smile faded when she saw who it was. This was the owner of Hawkins Yard – she'd never spoken to him – but had seen him once or twice when she visited Dan at his workplace.

Her heart was hammering so hard she thought it would escape from her bodice. She could think of only one reason why such an important gentleman would visit her house.

'Good afternoon, Mrs Cooper, might I be permitted to come in for a moment?'

Her mouth was too dry to answer; her tongue appeared to be stuck to the roof of her mouth. She gestured that he enter and directed him to the front parlour – the room they rarely used.

'There has been a most dreadful accident, Mrs Cooper, and I am the bearer of the most tragic tidings. Mr Cooper has been killed. I am most dreadfully sorry for your loss and give you my heartfelt condolences.'

She couldn't take it in. Dan couldn't be dead. She'd seen him only a few hours ago when he was getting dressed for work. Nobody had ever been killed at the yard since he'd worked there. It had to be a mistake.

Her head was cloudy; her mind couldn't make sense of his news. From a distance, she heard him say her name and then her knees buckled and she collapsed in a heap at his feet.

'Mrs Cooper, is there someone I can send for? You should not be alone at such a time as this. The accident wasn't Mr Cooper's fault and I will see that you and your family are recompensed.'

His last words finally penetrated the fog of her brain. She remained on the floor knowing her legs couldn't hold her upright at the moment. 'Nothing can recompense this family for the death of my husband and the father of my children. Send someone to my brother, Alfie Nightingale. He lives at twelve Maidenburgh Street. I need him and my sister-in-law to come here right away.'

8

The boys had had a good day and Alfie gave them a few extra coppers each for their hard work. He was just sitting down to a well-earned tea when somebody hammered at the front door.

'I'll get it, Betty love; you carry on feeding our Tommy.'

He opened the door to find a complete stranger waiting to speak to him. 'You Alfie Nightingale?'

He nodded. 'What you want?'

'Dan Cooper was killed this morning and you're wanted at the widow's house.' Having delivered his dreadful news the man put his cap back on and went about his business, leaving devastation behind him.

Alfie couldn't take it in. His best mate, his sister's man, had been lying dead under that pile of wood whilst he'd been nicking timber down the river. His stomach clenched and he reeled against the doorjamb.

'What's wrong, love? Who was that at the door?' Betty called from the kitchen.

Somehow he got his wits together, wiped his eyes on his sleeve, and stumbled back to give her the awful news.

'Get your things together; we've got to go to our Sarah. Her Dan's dead.'

Her face crumpled and she turned the colour of dough. 'Not Dan. I don't believe it. Sarah was so happy...' She couldn't go on. Tears were streaming down her cheeks and she was clutching their son so hard he began to wail in protest.

He gathered her into his arms and they cried together for a bit. 'We've got to go. The boys are still out back. I'll tell them what's happened. They'll need to keep an eye on this place whilst we're gone.'

* * *

Word must have spread as he got sympathetic nods, and the men doffed their caps solemnly as he and Betty hurried through the narrow streets and walks on their way to Greenstead. The second time she stumbled he was forced to put his arm around her, but she wouldn't let him take the baby.

'I'll carry our Tommy. I need to keep him close at a time like this.'

On the way there all Alfie could think was that Sarah hadn't just lost her beloved husband today, she'd likely lost her home as well. Even without the added burden of the second debt on the house, there was no way his sister could keep up the mortgage payments with no money coming in every week.

'I reckon they'll have to come and live with us, Betty love. Sarah will lose the house. The bailiffs will be in soon enough.'

'Couldn't we go and live with them instead? If you sold the cottage there'd be plenty of cash to tide us over...'

'It won't work. Dan took out a second mortgage to help us. I ain't earning enough to pay off his debts and everything else.'

She was rigid beside him as she took in his words. 'So Sarah's going to lose her lovely home because of us?'

'That's about right, Betty, but there ain't any point in telling her just now. We'll stay with her until after the funeral and then sit down and explain how things are. It'll be hard, all of us living in our little cottage – but better than the alternative.'

'I grew up with six of us in one bedroom. We'll manage. Sarah and her family must have the big room, and we'll move into the back room with Tommy.'

'Whatever you say, love. As long as we're together, and no one's heading for the workhouse, that'll be fine by me.'

She was flagging long before they reached Greenstead, so he insisted he carry the baby the rest of the way. When they approached the front gate he could see there were several people standing about outside in the road as well as another half a dozen in the garden itself.

Folk always rallied round when someone died – and Dan had been a popular gent, always ready to help someone out, to share what he had with those who had less. If they had stayed in the house at The Hythe things wouldn't be so dire; there wouldn't be the huge debts. He was sure Dan would still have lent him the money he'd put by, but he reckoned he could have kept both houses going and still paid off the debt.

No point in repining – he'd just have to do the best he could for his sister and her family. When she found out his part in all this she'd likely never forgive him. He came to a decision, not one he was happy with, but he had no choice.

'I'll be doing more work for Hatch in future, Betty love, or there won't be enough coming in to feed us all.'

'You do what you have to, Alfie – you'll get no complaints from me.'

Hopefully she would think he was talking about rent collecting, but he knew the extra work would involve nefarious activity.

Someone opened the gate for them and they walked in. The house didn't look the same no more – the joy had been taken from it. He didn't know any of the folk who were offering their condolences, and patting him on the back, but he nodded and smiled and thanked them.

The door was ajar and he pushed it open, expecting to hear his sister crying, but the house was silent.

'I'm in here, Alfie, in the parlour.'

This door was open too and he stepped in, shocked at the change in his Sarah. She seemed to have aged by ten years, but she was dry-eyed and seemed in control of her grief. He made to hug her but she flinched away.

'Betty, if you put Tommy down on the blanket over here, perhaps you would make tea for the kind people who have come around. I can't seem to get myself back on my feet at the moment.'

'I'll do that, love; you stop where you are. I brought a batch of biscuits with me. I'll take those out as well.'

His wife put little Tommy down and then hurried off to the kitchen. He took a seat opposite his sister. 'What time do the boys get back from school? Do they know yet?'

She stared at him as if she hadn't understood his words. She rubbed her hand across her eyes before she answered. 'I'd forgotten all about them. Can you go and fetch them from school? I don't want them to arrive here at the same time as Dan. They are bringing him up so he can be laid out properly. Someone from the yard brought me the news. He says he will take care of the funeral expenses. That was kind of him, wasn't it?'

'Least they can do. He were killed working for Hawkins and it weren't his fault neither. You should get compensation; they owe you that much. Dan worked there for fifteen years or more and deserves to be treated right.'

'I know it's true. I know that he's dead, but somehow I can't really believe it. I think when I see his body, I'll know it's true.' She waved vaguely towards the door. 'Could you put up a trestle in the best parlour so they have somewhere to put him when he comes? I think the man from Hawkins is sending round for the undertakers. I suppose we'll have the service at St Leonard's, where we got married, even though St Andrew's Church is a lot nearer.'

'I'll get onto that right away. Will you be all right with both babies in here?'

'Tommy is happy to play with his toes and Mary will be asleep for another hour at least.'

She weren't right – too quiet – too composed, but it took folk in different ways, grief did. He poked his head into the room nobody used and saw there was ample space for Dan to be laid out until he was buried.

Betty was clattering about in the kitchen and he went through to tell her what was going on. 'I'm that worried about her. It don't seem normal, not crying like.'

'She'll do plenty of that – don't worry about it, Alfie love. She's got to be strong for the boys, hasn't she?'

He was about to fetch the trestle when he remembered he was supposed to be fetching the boys first. He'd get a couple of the blokes from outside to take care of the table whilst he ran down to the school.

Once he'd organised that unpleasant task to his satisfaction, he took off for the school. Buster had remained behind. Animals seemed to have a sense of something being wrong and his dog was pressed close to his sister with his head in her lap, offering her what comfort he could.

The children would be coming out in half an hour and he

wanted to have the boys home before they heard about their pa's death from one of their cronies.

He went to the door of the classroom they was in and stood for a second or two gazing at a scene he hadn't seen for many years. The teacher was striding up and down at the front of the schoolroom – the children sat at their desks, the girls on the left, the boys on the right, in rows running to the very back of the large room. There must be more than fifty children in here, which were a lot for one man to educate properly.

The boys' side of the schoolroom started with the youngest at the front going back to the oldest. He could see John copying something carefully on his slate in the front row.

He knocked on the door and waited for the schoolmaster to open it.

'I beg your pardon for interrupting, sir, but I need the Cooper boys. Their pa's met with an accident and they need to be home with their ma.'

He nodded. 'If you care to wait here, I'll send them out to you.'

The poor little buggers would know something was up – the only time any child was allowed out of school early was for a family tragedy.

When they emerged, John was already crying, Davie was trying not to, and Joe was biting his lip. He knelt down and gathered them into his arms. 'I've got some right bad news for you, lads – your pa were killed at work today. I've come to take you home.'

It took quite a while for them to be composed enough to leave the schoolyard and head for Greenstead. John was big enough to walk but Alfie turned his back to the child. 'Here, hop on, I'll give you a piggyback. We'll be home quicker that way.'

Davie was clinging onto his trouser leg, Joe was holding his other arm. They'd lost their real ma a couple of years ago and now they only had Sarah to take care of them. No – he vowed he would look out for them in future – try and be a pa.

* * *

Sarah didn't know how long she'd been sitting on the floor when Tommy got his toes caught in his shawl and started to wail, which woke up Mary, who joined in. Sarah forced her legs to move and slid from the settle onto the floor beside the two babies. 'There you are, little one. No need to make such a fuss.' Tommy beamed at her – he was a happy little soul despite his precarious first few weeks.

Mary rolled over on her tummy and somehow staggered to her feet. 'Mama, Mama,' she babbled and held out her arms. Sarah reached out and embraced her daughter. 'Things will be different now, sweetheart, but we'll get through it somehow. Whatever happens, you still have your ma and your big brothers.'

Betty had brought her tea but this remained undrunk and was now cold. Her friend had closed the parlour door so she had her privacy and for that she was grateful. She couldn't face the sympathy and sad faces at the moment.

She pulled out the po from under the sideboard. 'Sit on this, Mary love. We don't want a puddle on the floor, do we?'

The baby was happy to comply. Keeping busy was the answer. As long as she was occupied she didn't have to think about what had happened. 'Good girl, we'll put this back and Ma will empty it later.' No sooner had she done this than the door opened and the three boys rushed in.

They flung themselves into her arms, knocking Mary over in their eagerness to be comforted. Alfie rescued the baby and she was content to be cradled in her uncle's arms.

'Ma, I want my pa back,' Davie sobbed. John was too upset to do anything more than bury his head in her shoulder. Joe recovered first.

'How will we manage? Where are we going to live now?'

'I don't know, love, but I promise you we will stay together whatever happens.'

Alfie crouched down beside them. 'Don't you fret, son; you can move in with us when you have to.'

'Thank you, I don't know what we'd do without you, Alfie.' Gently she removed the two youngest boys from her arms and lifted them onto the settle. 'Sit here. I need to get to my feet. Joe, will you keep an eye on your brothers and the babies for me?'

He straightened his shoulders. 'I'm the man of the house now, Ma. You can rely on me. I'll not go back to school but find myself a job.'

'Don't worry about it now, plenty of time to discuss such things after the funeral.'

Alfie put the baby down to play with his son on the floor and waited to be told what she wanted him to do next. Her mind was blank. There must be something important that needed doing but she couldn't think what it might be.

She scarcely had time to dry her face, shake out her skirts, and get to the door before four men appeared at the front gate carrying a shrouded shape on a trestle. Her knees almost buckled for a second time but she was determined to remain calm for the children.

She prayed there would be somebody amongst the neighbours who knew how to prepare a body for burial because she was certain she couldn't do it on her own. When her little brother had drowned all those years ago a neighbour had done what was necessary. She recalled that Tommy had been dressed in his best and looked as if he was asleep when she'd been allowed in to say her farewells.

'Auntie Betty will bring you in milk and biscuits. You must stay here and play quietly.'

Once outside the door she gripped her brother's arm. 'I must fetch his best clothes. We will probably need hot water and cloths, but I'm not really sure how to proceed.'

'You get what's wanted from upstairs and I'll take care of the rest. You don't have to do this, Sarah love. There'll be somebody here who knows what to do.'

She didn't want to see them bringing in the trestle. She wasn't even sure she could bear to look at Dan when he was laid out ready for his coffin. She certainly didn't want to see him mangled from his accident.

He could be buried in his wedding suit. As she was collecting the garments he would need, she hesitated. She wasn't stupid. She was certain they would be penniless by the time all the debts were paid – that all the lovely furniture, the chickens, the pig, everything she loved, would have to go. The only thing of value that would be left to sell would be Dan's personal possessions. Wouldn't it make more sense to dress him in something older and keep these items to sell?

People would talk, but they wouldn't be the ones facing destitution in a week or two. Decision made, she put the almost new clothes back in the closet and took out his second best. She was about to return when there was a soft tap on the door.

'Sarah love, can I come in?'

'Come in, Alfie. There's something I want you to do for me.'

When she told him she wished him to remove Dan's wedding ring and return it to her he didn't protest, but nodded. 'I'll do that right away. Give me them things. I'll take them down. You need to be with your children, not hiding away up here.'

'I'm coming. The boys will want something to eat. Biscuits and milk is all very well, but I need to get them something more substantial.'

'My Betty's taking care of that, Sarah love. All you've got to do is take care of the little 'uns and we'll do everything else.'

The rest of the day drifted past in a blur. Sarah focused her attention on the boys and the babies and after an hour or two you would scarcely have known such a tragedy had taken place in the household. Only Joe remained sombre; the other two were playing a quiet game of spillikins. Of course, Mary was too young to know what was going on.

By teatime the stream of visitors had stopped and the house was quiet – unnaturally so. She had eaten nothing all day, but the boys and the babies had eaten as usual. Betty sat next to her and took her hands and then spoke so quietly the children couldn't overhear what she said.

'The undertakers are here with the coffin. I think you and the boys should go and say goodbye before they nail the lid down.'

Her stomach plummeted. When she saw her beloved husband lying cold and still in his box she would have to accept he had left her forever. 'Joe, Davie, John, come with me.'

Obediently they stood up and quietly filed through the door behind her. A grand wooden coffin with brass handles stood open on the trestle. From the door she couldn't see into it and wasn't sure she wanted to. The boys hung back, clinging onto her skirts, and she wondered if it was sensible to make them see their father as he was.

The room was empty. The curtains were drawn out of respect but she could hear the shuffling feet of the undertakers in the front garden waiting for her to pay her respects so they could complete their task. Alfie had said Dan was to remain where he was until the morning and then three men from the timber yard, and himself, would be pallbearers. There was to be a horse-drawn hearse, and the wake would be held at the yard. Mr Hawkins was paying for everything – all she had to do was get herself and the children to the church and back.

She wished she could ask Mr Hawkins to give them the money instead of paying out for the unnecessary extravagance of an expensive coffin and hearse. He wouldn't agree. He wasn't doing this for her benefit but to show everyone what an upstanding citizen he was, and how well he looked after his employees and their families.

With her arms around the boys' shoulders she pushed them forward. Whoever had laid him out had done a good job. Dan looked as if he was asleep – like her little brother had. She hadn't asked where his injuries were and didn't want to know.

'Can we touch him? Will he wake up?' Davie whispered.

'You can touch him, love, but he won't wake up. He's gone to live with your ma in heaven.'

Joe snorted. 'Pa ain't going anywhere but in the ground. He shouldn't have died. We needed him here with us.'

'We did, sweetheart, but tragedies happen. We have just got to make the best of it and stay together whatever happens.'

The body she was looking at could have been anyone – it wasn't Dan any more. His skin was cold. She didn't want to be in here a moment longer.

'I think we should all go for a walk in the field with the dogs. They haven't been out all day.'

'I'll stop here, Ma. I don't want to leave him alone.' Joe's face was pinched, his eyes hard. He had grown up today and she would have to stop treating him in the same way as his younger brothers, and give him the respect he was due.

* * *

The children were in bed late and she was ready to follow them when Alfie asked her to stay. 'We need to talk, Sarah love, get things straight like, before tomorrow.'

'I know what's coming, Alfie; you don't need to tell me. Indeed, you have already said we must come and live in your little cottage or be on the streets or in the workhouse on Pope's Lane.' She sniffed and didn't bother to find her handkerchief. 'I think there's an alternative. I'll send word to my maternal grandparents and ask them if they would be prepared to take us in. The boys are old enough to help out with work on the farm and I can help as well.'

Alfie looked horrified but Betty didn't have time to hide her expression of relief. 'You can't do that – Dan wanted the boys to get a decent education. Maybe Joe's old enough to help out, but not Davie or John. We'll stick together – I'll not have you anywhere else but with me and Betty, and baby Tommy.'

'Let's not be hasty. I'll write to them and see what they say. Joe can help you with your deliveries until the matter's settled. Excuse me, I'm going to write my letter and then I'll retire. I just want tomorrow to be over.'

'I know, love. It weren't supposed to be like this. I were think-ing... I've sent word to me lads to fetch the barrows at dawn tomorrow. You need to pick the things you want to keep and we'll get them away from here before the bailiffs come.'

'Thank you. The children's beds, the cradle and my rocking chair. I should also like the things we were given as wedding gifts – and of course, all our personal belongings as well.'

Betty had been silent for some time – not something she was accustomed to doing. 'What about the chickens and the pig?'

'The neighbours have already taken them and given me a fair price,' Alfie said.

Then Sarah understood why the house had seemed even

quieter than it did when Dan was at work. Spot was no longer there.

'Who has taken our dog?'

'He's gone to a good home. He'll get plenty of runs in the fields and—'

She was on her feet. It wasn't her brother's place to sell their livestock and beloved pet. 'You will go at once and get him back. The boys have lost enough today and they are not going to lose their dog as well.'

For a moment, she thought he was going to refuse but then wisely thought better of it. 'No need to get uppity, Sarah; I was doing what I thought would be best for you. I'll fetch him back – but I don't reckon we'll be able to keep him, not indefinitely.'

'Which makes it even more imperative we move to Great Bromley. He will be invaluable on a farm and can earn his keep in a way that he couldn't ever do here.'

He went off not best pleased by her decision. 'I know you don't want us to live with you, Betty, but I hope you can put up with us until we can make other arrangements. The dog can live outside so you'll hardly know he's there.'

Her limbs were heavy as lead and her tongue too big for her mouth. Not waiting for a response from her friend, she dragged herself upstairs, too tired and grief-stricken to write the letter. It would have to be done first thing in the morning, before the funeral, if they were to have a settled home to go to.

9

Alfie was up at dawn and the furniture that was being taken to his cottage was already outside waiting to be put onto the carts when the boys arrived. They had got their pa to accompany them.

'Sad time, Alfie lad, thought you could do with a bit of a hand today but don't need no recompense – glad to help,' Fred Sadler said.

'Much appreciated. The more we can store in my sheds the better.'

He was relieved when they had gone as he didn't want any curious neighbours to report what had happened to the bailiffs when they eventually turned up – which they surely would.

He walked to the end of the plot and released the chickens and the pig for the last time. They would be collected whilst the family was attending the funeral. Spot shoved his cold, damp nose into his hand. 'I know, I shouldn't have done it. I'm glad you're back.'

He opened the gate that led out into the fields and the dogs bounded out. They'd better get accustomed to finding their own food as there wouldn't be any rhino spare to buy them nothing.

Then he recalled how he'd fed Buster when he'd been living as a street thief in London. He'd got rancid pies and such from the bakers, maggot-infested bones from the butchers, and his dog had thrived on this fare.

As he approached the kitchen window he saw someone moving about inside but couldn't tell if it was Betty or Sarah. He walked in through the scullery and found his sister setting the table for breakfast as if nothing was wrong.

It didn't do to bottle things up. She needed to cry, to grieve for the man she'd loved so much. He'd been miserable for weeks after Jim had died and that were only his best friend, not like losing a husband or child.

'I saw you coming, Alfie, and have your tea poured. I wasn't sure if I should use up the bacon or keep it...' She stopped and he made to comfort her but she shook her head. 'No, I'm not going to give in. Dan wouldn't want me to mope about.'

'That's all very well, Sarah love, but you've just lost your man. No one, not even the boys, expect you to put on a brave face today.'

She ignored his comment and pointed to a chair. 'I need to talk to you, get things straight before everyone else's up. I've written the letter to our grandparents but I'll not post it just now. I don't think things are quite as bad as I feared.'

He sipped at his tea and waited for her to continue. He should tell her about the loan, but didn't know how to break it to her.

'I know that we had some debts, that without the extra money Dan was making as your partner in the carpentry business we couldn't make ends meet. I also understand that even with no debts I couldn't continue to live there without an income.

'The money from selling the furniture, the pigs and chickens should cover anything we owe. This means the money Mr

Hawkins has promised us, and any money collected at the wake, will give us enough to rent our own cottage.'

'You have four mouths to feed and no husband to bring in the money.'

'I know that. I shall go to Mr Hyam – he employs women outworkers – and I'll earn something myself. Joe has said he's not going back to school and I'm hoping he will be able to earn a few pennies a day doing odd jobs for you and anyone else who needs him.'

Alfie swallowed the lump in his throat and prepared to tell her about the second mortgage Dan had taken out on his behalf. The bank would take every penny she had, including anything given to her by Mr Hawkins. She would be destitute, unable to rent her own cottage and be obliged to live with him in future.

'There you are. Your boys are getting themselves dressed in their Sunday best. I've changed Mary and she's clean and fresh.' Betty put their niece into her special chair and smiled at him. 'I'm going back to feed our Tommy. I'll be down shortly.'

The opportunity had gone. Maybe it was better Sarah didn't know the worst until she got through today. The bank would hear that Dan was dead and unable to meet his obligations sometime today, and might well swoop like black crows on the family before the day was out.

'I think you, Betty and the children should go back to the cottage after the wake. I'll stop down here with Buster and Spot and take care of what needs doing. You're best away from this.'

'Betty doesn't want us to move in with you...'

'She ain't got no choice in the matter. She'll do as she's told and get on with it.'

His sister flinched at his tone and he regretted speaking so harshly. 'She owes you, Sarah love. You stepped in and helped us when we needed it most and she can do the same for you. I've told the lads to come back to collect the remainder of your belongings so they need to be ready by the door. They'll be back before we leave.'

'I'll do it after breakfast. I thought I'd wrap our garments in the bed linen when everyone's up.' She glanced around the kitchen. 'There are still a lot of things on the shelves, in the pantry, and elsewhere that will be invaluable in the new cottage when I rent it. Hopefully your lads can bring a barrow up tomorrow or the next day.'

Alfie buried his face in his mug not wishing her to see his expression. Anything in the house when the bailiffs came would disappear to go towards the massive debt. Unless he could think of a way of hiding them, her garments and those of the children would also be taken and she'd be left with only what she was standing up in.

There was no time to discuss matters with his wife as Sarah and the boys were in the kitchen with them. Nobody had much appetite. Even Mary turned her little face away when Betty offered her bread and milk.

'Boys, the dogs have been out long enough. Why don't you go and call them back?' Alfie suggested. The children looked at their ma for permission and she nodded.

'Yes, run along, but you must stay clean and tidy. We will be leaving for the church in half an hour.'

'Have you got the bundles ready, Sarah love? I can hear my lads and their pa coming back. We might as well send as much as we can up now.'

The three barrows had just crossed Greenstead Road when the fancy hearse arrived outside the front gate. It were drawn by two black horses each with a matching ostrich plume attached to their bridles. The undertakers would transport the coffin to the vehicle – he and the other three wouldn't have to be pallbearers until they reached St Leonard's.

* * *

Sarah still had her black gown from the time she had been in mourning for Dan's first wife. It was a bit snug over the bosom but otherwise fitted well. She pinned on her bonnet and pulled down the veil.

Betty was wearing her normal clothes but had a black armband, as did the three boys. 'A few years back, Sarah, women didn't have to go funerals. I wish it was the same nowadays.'

'I want to go to pay my respects to Dan and it's important for the boys to see how much the neighbours, workmates and friends thought of their pa. I'm not looking forward to having to carry Mary all that way.'

Davie pulled at her skirt. 'Why can't she go in with our pa? He wouldn't be lonely then.'

'I'm afraid it's not done, sweetheart. I've made her a seat out of this shawl. She'll be comfortable in this and it will be easier for me to carry her.'

They were waiting in the family parlour for the coffin to be taken to the hearse before they ventured out. Probably the neighbours thought her cold-hearted not to be walking at the side of the wooden box. Dan was gone. Nothing she did would bring him back and she didn't care what anyone thought of her behaviour. The only person whose opinion she valued was dead. No that wasn't quite true – she still had her brother and she thanked the good Lord for that.

Alfie knocked on the door. 'It's time to go, Sarah love. Are you ready?'

How could she be ready to say goodbye to the man she'd

fallen in love with after they were wed? How could it be possible she was still only just nineteen years of age, the mother of four children and a widow?

The driver snapped his whip and the hearse moved off at a snail's pace. She and the boys walked directly behind. Alfie and Betty followed, and then anyone else who wanted to join the funeral procession tagged along after.

As they made their way to the church, passers-by came out and bowed their heads in respect. She looked neither to right nor left, but kept her eyes fixed on the coffin. There was an extravagant spray of lilies adorning it. Another unnecessary expense that would have been better put aside to help the boys.

Only then did she realise Mr Hawkins hadn't joined the cortège. Presumably he would appear at the church and expect to walk behind the coffin as if he had the right to be there.

The church bells were tolling when they arrived. Whilst she and the family waited, those who had walked slipped into the church. From the hum of conversation coming out of the open door the place was full.

Alfie and three men Dan had worked with at the yard for many years shouldered the coffin. The rector began to intone the funeral service as he led them into the dim interior. All through the service all she could think of was: why hadn't Mr Hawkins come to pay his respects? The words of the eulogy went over her head, she stood up and sat down when required, but didn't join in with the hymns.

Eventually it was over and the rigmarole was played out in reverse. Dan would have hated this and she'd had enough herself.

Alfie was a pallbearer again, of course, but Betty was walking beside her. 'I'm not going to the churchyard or to the wake. I'm taking the children to your cottage. Do you have the key?'

'No, Alfie has it. He'll not be able to give it to you until the interment's over.'

'Then I'll wait in the yard until you arrive to let me in. Surely his lads must have a key or they would have had to leave our belongings outside?'

Betty did her best to dissuade her from this unconventional behaviour but Sarah had made up her mind. The boys had suffered enough. They didn't need to see their pa going into the cold, dark ground.

'Joe, hold on to your brothers' hands and make sure they don't get in the way of other pedestrians.'

The three of them trooped along in front of her, too dispirited to take an interest in the diligences, carts and other interesting vehicles that were trundling up and down the hill.

'Shall we go and look at the castle before we go to our new home?'

'Why can't we go back to our proper house, Ma? I don't want to live with Uncle Alfie in his little cottage,' Davie whined.

'Shut yer gob, Davie. Don't you think Ma has enough to put up with today without you carrying on?' Joe said.

John was silent. He hadn't said a word since he'd heard the dreadful news yesterday. The only one in the family who was unbothered was Mary and for that Sarah was profoundly grateful. The boys might never get over the loss of their father, but his daughter would have no memory of him, which would probably make things easier for her.

By the time they reached the High Street, having trudged up Hythe Hill and Queen Street, they were all exhausted and she thought better of her suggestion to stop to look at the castle. None of them complained when she marched them past and straight down East Stockwell Street.

She was unsurprised to discover the side gate was open and

that the yard was occupied. The boys perked up a bit and ran ahead to investigate. When she got in there it was to find the back door of the cottage open, and Fred Sadler just exiting.

'Morning, Mrs Cooper, didn't expect to see you here so soon. Me and the boys have got started upstairs like what your Alfie said to do.'

'You go down on the floor now, Mary, like a good girl. Your big brothers will take care of you for a bit.'

John managed a weak smile and took the toddler's hand in his. Joe and Davie just stood there waiting to be told what to do. 'Come in with me, boys,' Sarah said. 'You can help get our new room ready. It's going to be a bit of a squash, but better than the workhouse.'

The children pressed close to each other, their eyes wide with fright. She wished the intemperate words back, but it was too late to retract them. It would do no harm for them to understand that however difficult it was going to be sharing a small cottage, the alternative would be far worse. Not that there was any danger of them being destitute – but they had no concept of hardship, of deprivation, had lived a comfortable life up until now.

She knew only too well that things could change in an instant and one could find oneself thrown from a life of comfort to one of degradation and poverty.

The bundles of clothing and bed linen were piled neatly on the settle in the front parlour. The banging and clattering going on upstairs must mean Mr Sadler and his sons were in the process of putting the boys' beds together again.

When she looked into the larger front bedroom a little later, she saw two of the beds had been placed end to end under the window and the third was at right angles. The three horsehair mattresses were piled on one of the beds waiting to be put in place.

There was just room for the large bed, but the chest of drawers had gone. Mary would have to sleep beside her with a bolster on the edge to stop her rolling onto the floor. God knows where they would put their clothes – but they would manage because they had no choice.

Dickie and Bill were knocking in the last pegs that held the third little bed together. 'Almost done now, Mrs Cooper,' said their father. 'We've just got to move the bed next door.'

Sarah opened her mouth to protest that then she and Mary would have nothing to sleep on; but if she kept it then her brother and Betty would be in the same position. She would have to sleep on the boards. Mary was too big for her cradle so would have to top and tail with John.

'I'm glad you're all here and I thank you for your able assistance.'

'It ain't no trouble, Mrs Cooper – the least we could do. We ain't sure where you and the little one are going to sleep. Is there another bed coming?'

'We shall manage. Alfie will knock something up for us in a day or two.' She retreated downstairs as there was scarcely enough room for the four boys and Mr Sadler without her getting in the way. Hopefully there would be sufficient spare bedding for her to make up a rudimentary mattress upon which to sleep.

By keeping busy with a variety of mundane tasks she was able to get through the next two hours without breaking down. If she let her emotions get the better of her she would be letting down the children and not be able to deal with what might come next.

Joe went with his brothers to the baker to buy them all a pasty and a bun for their midday repast. Dickie, Bill and their father had long since departed and she had seen no sign of Alfie's neighbours even though she'd knocked on the door.

Mary, exhausted by pottering about outside with her brothers, flopped onto the dirt and fell asleep. 'Look at her, Ma, she don't care. Shall I bring her in? I can carry her up and she can go into my bed,' Joe said.

'No, she's so dirty she might as well stay where she is. I'll fetch you a rug. I'd be grateful if you would put her on that. I don't want her to wake up and start eating the dirt again.'

When her daughter was comfortably settled the boys insisted she went upstairs to see what they'd been doing whilst she'd been busy preparing the evening meal for the seven of them. She thought it would be safe enough to leave the sleeping baby for a few minutes.

'Look, Uncle Alfie and Auntie Betty will be right comfortable now we've got it all sorted for them. There's even room for the chest of drawers and the cradle,' Davie told her.

'I can see you've been very busy. I want you to promise me something, boys: you must always remember this isn't our house. We are guests here and must behave accordingly. Hopefully, we'll be able to rent ourselves a cottage and I can work as a seamstress whilst Joe helps Alfie with his deliveries. Money will be scarce, but we won't starve.'

John tugged on her skirt but didn't speak. 'Do you want me to come and see where we'll be sleeping, son?'

He nodded and pulled her in the direction of the front bedroom. 'My word, what a transformation you have made. I didn't know you'd found me a mattress. I shall be perfectly comfortable on that.' She pointed at John's bed, which now had a pillow at each end. 'I see you have got a place ready for your sister, John. Did you remember to put the piece of mackintosh at her end?'

'We did, Ma, and the draw sheet over it,' Davie said.

'You've thought of everything. Remember, loves, as long as we are together nothing else matters. Your pa would want you to be brave and strong and turn into young men he can be proud of.'

'Will Uncle Alfie be back soon?' Davie asked. 'We want to take the dogs for a run along the river and don't want to go without him.'

'I expect he'll be here before teatime. I've got some laundry to peg out whilst it's still sunny. There's not enough room for you to play up here. You can either do something quiet in the yard or the parlour.'

'Dickie's calling for us. He's going to show us around.' Joe sounded surly, not at all like his cheerful self. He was so like Dan it broke her heart to look at him.

'Don't stay out too long, and make sure that John doesn't wander off.'

'He ain't coming with us; he wants to stop here with you and the baby,' Joe said. 'It don't seem right somehow. We're going about our daily business and Pa only died yesterday. I don't reckon you care that he's gone. You're not our real ma anyway. She would have shown more respect and gone to the burial and cried for him.'

She was stunned by his outburst but he was gone before she could respond. John was still enveloped in her skirts, clinging on to her leg like a lifeline. Dan had only been gone for a day and already she was saying and doing the wrong things.

'You have to let go of me, John. I can't go downstairs with you attached to my leg. We can sit on the step together whilst Mary sleeps.'

She blinked her eyes. It was as if there was sand in them. Her throat was raw and her arms and legs were too heavy to move. Running away from the burial and the wake had been a dreadful error of judgement and she feared Joe might never forgive her.

10

Alfie noticed his sister and the boys had gone as he stood by the open grave watching his friend be lowered into the dirt. When the rector had finished, he stepped back until he was able to speak to Betty.

'Where are they? They should be here. Folk will think it strange the widow ain't at the graveside.'

'She's taken the boys to our cottage. She wanted the key. I told her I didn't have one, but she went anyway.'

'The cottage's open – Fred and the lads are moving stuff about so it's ready for later. Make sure you tell everyone at the wake she was taken poorly – I'll do the same.'

It were a brisk walk to the timber yard where Mr Hawkins was putting on a spread for Dan. The bloke should have been here himself – Sarah wasn't the only one whose absence had been noted.

He stuck it out for an hour and then decided he too had had enough. The mourners seemed to have forgot why they were there and the atmosphere had become like a party. It were as if Dan hadn't died at all.

He took Betty's arm and drew her to one side. 'You get off up to the cottage and help Sarah and the boys settle in. I've got to go back to the house and see to some business but I'll be home before dark.'

'I'm coming with you, Alfie. I need to give the place a good clean before the bank repossesses it. Do you think they will come for the furniture and stuff today?'

'I reckon so. I'm hoping the pig and the chickens have already gone. I left the dogs roaming free in the house to stop the bailiffs from breaking in.'

He didn't bother to say farewell. No one was interested in anything but free food and drink. He stopped on the quay where the accident had taken place, but there was nothing to show for it. The barges had gone; the timber was safely stacked in the yard. When a bloke died it was like dropping a stone into the river – a few ripples and then nothing to show for his life.

Betty kept nattering on but he'd learnt over the months to ignore her and didn't bother to listen until she forced him to.

'Alfie, what do you think? Did I do right?'

'Do right? I ain't been listening. What are you on about?'

'Sarah wrote the letter to her grandparents. She put the penny stamp on, but left it on the dresser in the kitchen. I posted it for her.'

'You shouldn't have done that; it weren't none of your business. You need to keep your nose out of our affairs in future.' No sooner had he spoken than he regretted the turn of phrase. Betty looked stricken, as if he'd struck her.

'I see. You put your sister and her family ahead of your own wife and son. Small wonder you invited them to live with us regardless of my opinion. Now I know where I stand, Alfie Nightingale, and I wish I'd never met you.'

She snatched her arm away from him and marched off

towards the bridge that would take her over the river and back into the heart of Colchester. He were too miserable to call out, to try and make amends, but he'd put things right between them later when Sarah didn't need him so much.

He'd only moved into the marital bed a week or so ago and now he regretted having done so. The way his luck was running, she would be expecting again, and the last thing he wanted was another bleedin' baby. Tommy was enough for him and he'd promised himself he would be a father to Dan's children as well.

As he neared the house in Greenstead he increased his pace. The noise of the dogs barking and howling told him the bastards were already there to take everything what was left.

He remained stony-faced as a legal crow handed him the papers that gave the ownership of the house back to the bank and all the contents also. They wouldn't let him go in again. He collected both dogs and began the long walk to Maidenburgh Street.

He weren't given to asking favours of the Almighty, in fact he thought it unlikely there was a God of any sort. If there were, he were a rotten bugger. He let people die and bad things happen to good folks and had never answered none of his prayers, that was for sure.

He walked back along the river and by the time he was in his own neighbourhood he'd calmed down a bit, was ready to face the wrath of both his wife and sister. He just hoped that Betty hadn't already told Sarah the true state of affairs, that her fury at his comment hadn't prompted her to break her promise to him.

As he left the water meadow he saw all three of his nephews messing about with Dickie and Bill. It were as if he'd swallowed a stone; a weight pressed into his chest at the memory of that dreadful day when his little brother had drowned at this very place a few years back.

'Look, Buster, Spot, look who's there. Go on, lads, find the boys.'

The dogs didn't need telling twice but raced off barking in excitement. This was what he'd hoped they'd do. The five lads immediately moved away from the bank, from danger, and turned to fling their arms around the massive animals as they arrived beside them.

'What are you lot doing down here? Does your ma know you've come to the river?'

Joe scowled. 'She ain't our ma, and you ain't no uncle neither. We're orphans and we can do what we bleedin well like.'

Alfie reacted without thinking. He snatched the boy up by the scruff of his neck and gave him a good walloping. 'Don't you ever talk to me like that. You're my responsibility now and you'll give me the respect you gave your pa.' He gave the boy another shake to emphasise his words.

The other boys were staring open-mouthed but didn't seem unduly bothered by his actions. He dropped Joe back to his feet and waited for the boy to run off. That's what he would have done. Instead Joe scrubbed his eyes with his hands and grinned.

'My pa never raised a hand to us – but I reckon he'd have given me a lot worse than you did if he'd been here.'

'We'll say no more about it, Joe lad. Now, Bill, Dickie, I need you bright and early tomorrow. Wednesday's the busiest day of the week – it being market day.'

The lads scampered off leaving him with his nephews. John took one hand and Davie took the other – Joe squared his shoulders and marched along in front as if nothing untoward had taken place. Alfie looked down at the two littlest. 'I never really hurt him. I don't reckon he'll even have a bruise on his arse.'

Davie looked up at him admiration in his eyes. 'It would serve him right if he did have. He's been right horrible all day and saying dreadful things about our ma.' The boy sniffed. 'We ain't orphans; we got you and Ma and Auntie Betty to take care of us now.'

'I don't reckon your ma would take too kindly to me dishing out a hiding to Joe, but too late to take it back. I'm not having none of you disrespect your ma, nor me, nor your Auntie Betty. It's been a bleedin' awful day and I'll be glad to get to bed.'

Joe had slowed his pace and appeared to be listening. 'I need some extra boys to earn a few pence tomorrow but I don't reckon I'll find anyone decent.'

The boy stopped but didn't turn his head. 'You've got me, Uncle Alfie. Will I do?'

'You'll do fine, son. You be up first thing and go along with Bill. He ain't too clever, but he's a strong lad. I reckon you'll get twice the work with you there to drum up trade.'

Although Spot hadn't visited the cottage he was happy to trek through the gate after Buster. They could sleep outside in future, or curl up in his workshop in a couple of sacks when it were cold.

Joe was talking to his brothers and they nodded before running up the steps. The boy turned to him. His face was tear-stained, but he looked remarkably cheerful considering. 'I ain't going to tell if you ain't. Ma don't need to know nothing about what happened.'

'It's up to you, son. You deserved it, but it'll not happen again. My Sarah don't hold with physical punishment and I'll not go against her wishes a second time.'

'I've had the strap a few times at school and none the worse for it. I'll mind my manners in future, don't you worry.' Joe paused. 'I can't imagine life without my pa. He was the world to us...' He couldn't complete the sentence and Alfie reached out and gathered him close.

The boy sobbed in his arms and he looked up to see Sarah

and Betty watching from the window. The girls seemed on good terms so maybe he'd been worrying unnecessarily.

There weren't enough room for everyone to sit round the table at the same time so the little ones were fed first and then sent to the yard to play. The babies were already asleep upstairs.

'Did anyone remark on my absence, Alfie? It all got too much for me.'

'One or two said something, but when I told them you was taken poorly they was sympathetic. We need to talk about what's going to happen next, Sarah love, but let's have supper first.'

He glanced at Betty and raised an eyebrow. She shook her head. If she'd said nothing, maybe it would be best to leave the bad news about her true financial state until the morning when they'd all had a good night's sleep.

Even his wife was quiet this evening. The absence of Dan weighed heavy on all of them. It were worse for Sarah, of course, but he'd meant a lot to him and Betty too.

'Why don't you go up, Sarah. I'll do the dishes as you prepared the food. I'll get in the laundry; I reckon it'll be dry by now.'

His sister stood up like an old woman, holding on to the edge of the table for support. 'I'll will go up, thank you, Betty. I know it's difficult having us all here, but hopefully it will only be temporary and I'll be able to find somewhere for us in the next few days. What with the money I've got put by, not much I know, and what Mr Hawkins has promised, I think I'll be able to manage as long as I find some work from Mr Hyam.'

When she'd gone he pointed to the yard and Betty followed him out. It wouldn't do to speak in the kitchen as every word said there could be heard upstairs.

'It's worse than we thought, Betty love. Them bank bastards took every penny from the collection and the five guineas Mr Hawkins donated. Sarah's got nothing. She won't be able to move and she'll be devastated when she finds out it were all my fault.'

'It wasn't your fault. You couldn't help being attacked and having to borrow money. Do you think you can use your tools now and get some furniture made?'

'I can do the planing, sawing and such, but not nothing else. I'm going to have to rely on the rent collecting I get from Hatch to provide for us all. I can knock up a few more baby chairs, tables and benches, but that's about the lot. No more dressers, beds or sideboards – my hand won't deal with that.'

'If you can keep the barrows busy, do more for Mr Hatch, then we should survive. I know it's going to be difficult having so many under one roof, but we'll manage.'

'You're a good wife to me, love, and I'm sorry I was riled with you for posting that letter.'

Whilst he locked up, checked the dogs had a full bowl of water and a bone each to gnaw on, Betty deftly folded the clean laundry and carried the basket in on one hip. Womenfolk liked to wash on a Monday but he reckoned with two babies, three boys, and three adults under his roof the copper would be going most days. God knows how they'd manage in the winter when they couldn't hang linen outside.

That night, despite his determination not to start another baby, when Betty pressed herself against him his body responded. Even the thought that his sister and the boys could hear every grunt and groan, every creak of the bed, didn't stop him.

* * *

The boys were sleeping soundly. The soft snuffling as they breathed reassured Sarah that they would get over this tragedy. It was a worry that John had yet to speak, but he seemed pleased when he'd discovered Mary sleeping at the foot of his bed. As usual the baby was on her hands and knees with her bottom in the air.

Despite being worn to the bone she couldn't rest. Every time she closed her eyes she saw Dan's body in the coffin and she couldn't bear it. Her throat was clogged, her eyes gritty, but she daren't give in to her grief and wake the house. Instead she scrambled up from her paillasse on the floor, picked up her shawl, and crept barefooted downstairs. Alfie didn't bother to lock the back door when the dogs were in the yard so there were no noisy bolts to pull back.

Neither dog bothered to get up, but both thumped their tails on the dirt as she stepped over them and went into the workroom. Fortunately, there was sufficient moonlight for her to see without stubbing her toes or cutting her feet on the debris of sawdust, broken nails and slivers of wood that littered the floor.

There was an upturned orange box that would serve as a stool. She moved into the far corner so she could rest her back against the wall and collapsed onto it. Finally, after holding back her tears for two days she gave in to her misery. She used her shawl to mop her eyes and it was sodden by the time she shuddered to a close.

'Good boys, have you come to comfort me?' Both dogs had come in and were pressed close to her, their warmth helping her regain her composure. 'I can't sit out here all night. I must go in and try and get some sleep. I'm sure tomorrow will not be any better than today.'

As she carefully picked her way into the yard the dogs followed her. If she found them a comfort, then she was sure the boys would also. She wondered if Joe knew just how like Dan he was – would he find it hard looking in the glass and seeing not just his own reflection, but the image of his dead father?

The animals made no attempt to go up the steps behind her,

but flopped down in the yard as before. She had heard the church clock strike two a while ago. With luck she would get a few hours' rest before Mary demanded her attention.

Alfie had said he was going to be out early, and wanted Joe to be ready when he did. She would get up herself and make them breakfast before they left for a hard day's work pushing the carts about the place delivering items folk had bought at the weekly market.

She stayed away from the High Street on Saturdays when the livestock sale took place, as the smell coming from the cattle, sheep and pigs that were penned at one end of the street was quite overwhelming. The Wednesday market was more pleasant as the local smallholders and farmers came in to sell their surplus produce. No doubt Betty would want to go and buy fruit, vegetables and eggs at some point during the day.

She would much prefer to remain in the cottage and not have to speak to anyone, to see the sympathetic looks, the sad faces of the neighbours. She could look after the little ones and let Betty do the purchasing this time.

Although she was exhausted, sleep eluded her and when the clock struck four she abandoned her attempt to rest and by the light filtering in through the window quickly got dressed. If she was up she would make herself useful, fill the copper with water and get it heating so they could get a load of laundry on later. She would also set some dough to rise so they could have fresh bread for breakfast.

The one advantage of being cloistered so close together was that she could hear if any of the children awoke and needed her. At dawn she heard Alfie creeping about in the room above the kitchen and then Joe must have got out of bed as she could hear sounds from the front room as well.

Yesterday's bread was sliced and waiting to be toasted but

there was no butter. They would have to make do with jam until Betty did her marketing today.

'Morning, Sarah love. Couldn't you sleep?' asked Alfie.

'No, I'm sure I'll catch up tonight. Sit down. The tea's brewed, but there's no butter or milk.'

'Don't need it, Ma, as long as there's sugar,' Joe said cheerfully as if his outburst the previous day had never taken place.

The boy gulped down his breakfast as if it might be the last meal he had and was outside to take the dogs for their morning constitutional whilst Alfie was still eating. This suited her as she wished to speak to him alone.

'I didn't have a chance to ask you, how much did I get from Mr Hawkins and the collection from Dan's workmates?'

He seemed not to have understood her question and she was about to repeat it when Mary began to call out. 'I'm sorry, I'll have to see to her. I'll talk to you when I come down.'

However, when she got back a quarter of an hour later the kitchen was empty and there was no sign of her brother anywhere. Then she had no time to dwell on his disappearance as Betty and the other two boys arrived in the kitchen and she was busy serving breakfast.

Half an hour later peace reigned and she was able to sit down and snatch a cup of tea and a piece of toast herself. Betty was delighted with her suggestion that she go to the market without Tommy today.

'I'll go off now, if you don't mind, Sarah love. You get the best bargains first thing and last thing. John's in the yard but Davie went off with Dickie and his cart.'

'John can entertain Mary and Tommy whilst I finish the bread. When the babies are having their morning nap I can get the first load of washing out. I don't know how we're going to manage if it rains.'

'You can get a fair bit on the rack up there, but it's better for airing than for drying – otherwise you get drips down your neck when you're eating your tea.'

Later the cottage was quiet. John was sitting at the table playing with some bits of wood he'd found in the yard, the babies were upstairs sleeping, when there was a bang on the front door.

11

Sarah was reluctant to open the door and decided to ignore it. The knocking ceased and she clenched her fists and continued with the ironing. Betty only had one flat iron but Alfie had thought to bring hers so she was able to have one heating on the range whilst she used the other.

Both dogs had gone with Alfie and the boys. If they hadn't, she would have had some warning that there was someone in the yard. The first she knew was when an elderly woman appeared in the open doorway.

'You didn't answer the door. I had to come round the back and that's not right.' The woman who spoke was tall and spare, her grey hair scraped back in an unforgiving bun. Her eyes were sharp and her mouth thin – but Sarah knew at once who she was.

'I beg your pardon, ma'am, I've been avoiding my neighbours. Please, won't you come in and take a seat?'

'Your grandpa and I heard that your man had been killed and that you are living here with your brother and his wife. We are sorry for your loss.'

'Thank you, your sympathy is much appreciated.' Sarah

hastily removed the ironing blanket and replaced the iron on the range. She bundled the rest of the laundry back into the basket to make room for her grandmother to sit at the table. Then she checked the water in the kettle was boiling and added two spoons of tea to the pot before tipping in the water.

'Where are your boys? I wanted to see them.' The old lady pulled out a chair and perched on the edge of it. 'How old are they?'

This was a strange request as the children weren't blood relatives, whereas she hadn't enquired after Mary at all. 'John is in the other room, he's six years. Davie and Joe are out working with their uncle. They are nine and ten years of age. Their sister, Mary, is...'

'Are they hard-working boys? Strong and healthy?'

Now Sarah understood the reason for this inquisition. Her grandmother wasn't interested in them as relatives, but as potential workers for the farm. She hadn't taken to this woman, and was glad the letter hadn't been posted and she and her family would not be obliged to move to Great Bromley.

'I asked you a question, young lady, and I expect a civil answer.'

'My sons are well-mannered, intelligent, diligent boys and a credit to their parents.' She wished now she hadn't invited this objectionable old woman to be seated. She certainly didn't intend to offer her a cup of tea.

'Thank you for calling by, Mrs Siddons, and I wish you good day.'

'I'll take a cup of tea seeing as you've made it for me.'

Sarah had no choice but to do as she was instructed. She handed the cup and saucer to her grandmother and sat down opposite with one of her own.

'We can offer you and your family a home if you need it, girl.

You'll get board and lodging but will have to work for it. You'll not want to stop here for long. You'd do better coming to us and making a fresh start.'

'Thank you for your offer. I will give it serious consideration.'

John slid in from the parlour to stand beside her chair. He didn't speak but was leaning into her, needing her warmth for reassurance.

'Is he touched in the attic? Doesn't he speak?'

'He's very upset to have lost his beloved pa. Once he has recovered from his grief he'll be as sunny-natured and talkative as always.'

The old lady slurped her tea and replaced the cup with a rattle in the saucer. 'Children are better seen and not heard, in my opinion, so being quiet is a good thing.' She stood up smartly, remarkably agile for a person of her age. 'I'll take my leave now, Sarah. I expect to hear from you in a week or two.'

Sarah was on her feet and managed to pull her mouth into a resemblance of a smile. 'Please convey my best wishes to my grandfather. Goodbye, ma'am.'

The woman snorted but said no more. Sarah held her breath until she heard the back gate close and knew they were alone again.

'Well, John, that was a surprise, wasn't it? That was your great-grandma and my grandma.' She couldn't think of anything polite to say about the unexpected visitor so changed the subject. 'Would you be a good boy and go upstairs and see if the babies are waking?'

He nodded and somehow managed to climb the uncarpeted staircase without making a sound. He was taking Dan's death harder than the rest of them and she prayed his silence, and subdued behaviour, would pass when the rawness of his loss had eased a bit.

She was glad she hadn't posted the letter – living with that woman was not something she would relish. Having met Mrs Siddons, she finally understood why her own ma had run away from the farm with the first young man she had met, and why she had never made any effort to resume contact with her parents.

In the bustle of the remainder of the day she was able to forget about the visit. It wasn't until she was sitting at the kitchen table with Alfie and Betty, after all the children had retired, that she had a moment to tell them what had transpired.

When she had finished, there was an uncomfortable silence and her brother and his wife exchanged glances. There was something going on that she was not privy to and an unpleasant sinking feeling enveloped her.

'Tell me what's wrong. I need to know. I don't want any secrets between us.'

'It's like this, Sarah love. Betty posted that letter yesterday and they'll have received it today.'

She was about to tell her friend exactly what she thought of this behaviour when he held up his hand.

'No, that's not the worst of it.'

When he had finished explaining she was too shocked to comment. She was destitute. There was no money at all apart from the few shillings she had in her purse. Either they remained as unwanted guests with Alfie and Betty, or moved to Great Bromley to live with her unpleasant grandparents.

'Sarah love, you ain't going to live with them. You'll stay here in Colchester and let me take care of you. Dan wouldn't want you and the boys to go there,' Alfie said.

'I know I wasn't too happy about the thought of sharing with you, but I'll not have you living with that woman,' Betty added. 'We'll make this work and maybe in a year or two we can sell this place and buy something bigger to accommodate us all more comfortably.'

'If you're sure, Betty, then I would love to stay. I'll go down and speak to Mr Hyam at his factory in Queen Street tomorrow and arrange to start doing piecework for him. If we sell the remainder of my furniture, Alfie, you can use the money to buy another barrow and my boys can work with that. You made a good living in London with only two of you and we can make it work between us.'

The weeks drifted past and gradually everyone adjusted to life without Dan – apart from John who still refused to speak. Alfie didn't buy a third cart as there just wasn't enough work to call for it. This meant the boys were kicking around by the river, or in the yard and the less salubrious parts of town, with nothing to do. Sarah had been equally unsuccessful obtaining sewing work from the factory and this left him with the burden of providing for this large family himself.

The furniture that Sarah had asked him to sell had been polished and made to look like new again. This would bring in a pound or two but wouldn't keep the wolf from the door for very long. Sarah and Betty were beginning to get on each other's nerves – were finding sharing the house and the kitchen right difficult.

The nights were getting darker and colder. It would be winter soon and the tension in the cottage could only get worse then. Reluctantly Alfie came to the conclusion there was only one alternative – he would agree to Hatch's request to become involved in his less legal activities. He'd been doing a bit of debt collecting, using Buster to terrify the poor blokes into paying up, but so far had refused to do anything dishonest.

'It's good money, Alfie lad, for the right bloke. For this you must leave that dog of yours behind – not the sort of work we want him around.'

'He'll not like it – but I reckon you're right. Can't risk him barking at a cat and alerting the constables. When do you want me?'

'There's a warehouse got a load of silk and such being delivered in the next day or so. You need to go down there and see what's what. A smart gent like you won't turn any heads – but leave the bleedin' dog behind like what I told you.'

'Where is it?'

'Down The Hythe – you're known there, you go for timber on a regular basis. You need to order some wood or somethink, then take a stroll around the place what I'm interested in. I need to know how many they've got on the door, how many works there, what sort of padlock they've got on the door.'

'Then I need to take Buster with me. I never go down that way without me dog. I'll leave him at home when we do it.'

He wanted to know exactly how the burglary would take place but thought it best if he didn't ask. Hatch would tell him when the time was right. He'd vowed never to earn money dishonestly again but here he was, about to help Hatch with a robbery. If Sarah or Betty ever found out they would disown him, so he'd better make sure they never did.

He thought he might as well take the three boys with him, get them out of the house for a bit and give the womenfolk a bit of peace and quiet.

'Where we going, Uncle Alfie?' Joe asked.

'Down the river – I've got to do a bit of business at the timber yard and then we'll walk along the wall with the dogs. Get your ma to pack us up a bit of bread and cheese and an apple or two and we'll have a bite to eat.'

Davie was inside like a rat from a drainpipe and Alfie could hear him making his request. John was sitting on the dirt playing with a pile of stones. It were worrying that the lad were still silent after so long. 'You coming with us, John lad? Be a nice treat. I reckon it'll be the last time we get to have a picnic this year.'

The boy shook his head and didn't answer. 'Fair enough – but if you ain't coming with me you get off your arse and go in and see if you can be a help to your auntie or ma. It's doing no one no good you sitting about here playing like a babe in arms.'

The child scrambled to his feet and ran indoors. Somethink had to be done to jerk the boy from his silence. It weren't natural him hanging about Sarah and Betty like this. There weren't the money to pay for them to go to the school any more and being taught his letters at home weren't the same.

He saw Sarah at the window. 'I'm taking the boys down the river. We'll be back before dark. Can't persuade John to come with us. You need to tell him sharpish that he's got to stop moping about.'

'I wondered why he ran upstairs. No point me asking him. He'd have to be dragged out kicking and screaming, and that won't do anyone any good. I know it's been more than a month since Dan died, but he needs longer to get accustomed to the idea.'

Betty appeared at the door with a linen bag bulging with sandwiches. 'Here you are, love – no need to hurry back.'

'Thank you, love. Dickie and Bill will be back before we are. Tell them to hand over the money and I'll pay them tomorrow.'

'Right you are, Alfie.'

The noise and smell of the livestock coming from the High Street made the yard unpleasant. Saturday market wasn't as good for deliveries as the Wednesday one, but there would be enough to keep the two smaller barrows busy.

Whilst he was waiting he'd slipped a piece of rope around the necks of both dogs. He weren't taking no chances not when there was beasts in the pens for them to chase. 'Here, Joe, you take your Spot; I'll hold Buster. We can let them go when we're away from the market.'

'I've got some root beer,' Davie said as he waved a second bag above his head.

'Then we'll get off. It gets dark by five o'clock so we'll want to be home before then.' Sensibly the boys had got on their mufflers as well as their thick coats so should be warm enough even with the brisk wind coming off the water.

They hadn't been down The Hythe since Dan's funeral and he were concerned about how they might react. He was going to get his wood from a yard in Barrack Street in future – a lot nearer even if it were more costly. He wouldn't be comfortable going into Hawkins Yard any more.

Davie carried the two bags with the sandwiches and ginger beer, Joe led his dog and he had Buster. The stink from the livestock made his nose curl; the smell never really went as it stuck between the cobbles, however many times it was scrubbed and swept. Folk were refusing to bring their carriages into the centre of town because running over the cobbles was uncomfortable and ruined the vehicles.

Maybe the council would do something about it before the centre of Colchester lost many of its businesses as the ladies began to shop elsewhere. What with the trains taking them to London, he reckoned they could go there easy enough nowadays.

The customs warehouse was on the opposite side of the river to Hawkins Yard and the coal yards, lime kilns and corn merchants, which all belonged to William Hawkins. In fact, he owned everything along that side of the river.

The tide was low, little activity on the dock, and the dogs were able to roam about sniffing out rats and suchlike to their hearts' content.

'When are we going to have our picnic, Uncle Alfie?' Davie asked. 'These blooming bags ain't half heavy.'

'I told you, we're going to walk through the docks and onto the river wall. We'll walk as far as that old hut. We can shelter in there from the wind. It's right parky today.'

As he strolled past the customs warehouse he had ample time to check the access points, how many guards there were, but he could hardly go around the back to check the rear of the building where the goods would be stored. Then fortune smiled on him as a mangy cat caught the eye of both dogs and they chased it into the yard of the customs warehouse barking and howling fit to wake the dead.

He and the boys dashed after them and the servants standing watch were only too happy to have them catch the massive beasts and remove them before they savaged anyone.

'Cor, look at that! That ain't the only thing chased up a wall,' Joe said, and he and his brother laughed. The welcome sound was one that hadn't been heard since their pa passed away.

The two blokes given the task of watching the back entrance had scrambled up a pile of packing cases and were peering out from behind them.

'You get them bleeding dogs out of here – they ain't safe around decent folks.' The man who spoke was of florid complexion, stout build and his companion was of similar appearance.

'Sorry, mate, they're after the cat what has gone up the tree. They don't bite unless I tell them to,' Alfie said cheerfully.

'I'll get them, Uncle Alfie. They're making such a racket they'll never hear you call,' Joe said as he dashed off, his brother in tow.

Whilst the boys collected the dogs and put them back on their leashes he took the opportunity to have a good look round whilst assisting the two guards back to the cobbled yard.

'Sorry for the disturbance. We'll be on our way. I reckon your cat will come down in an hour or two.'

'It ain't our cat – the master don't hold with no pets even though we could do with a couple to keep the rats down inside,' one of the blokes said cheerfully. 'Ain't had so much excitement in months. Fine dogs you got there, mister, and no harm done.'

'You don't store perishables here, so can't think what they'd be finding to eat,' Alfie replied.

'Them bleeders gnaw on everythink. Don't seem to matter; they eat the silk if they can get it.'

Alfie touched his cap and wandered out of the yard, well pleased with the encounter. 'Well done, lads, and you didn't even drop your bags, Davie.'

* * *

They returned at dusk tired with their excursion. The boys had laughed and played the fool all the way back – Alfie believed they were over the worst. There was a definite nip in the air, and the trees were already losing their leaves. The cold nights and icy winds were just around the corner.

The dogs had become accustomed to sleeping in his workshop and neither of them made any attempt to come inside any more. As long as they were fed, exercised and got a bit of fuss from the boys they were content.

The oil lamp was burning brightly in the centre of the kitchen table and his baby son and his cousin Mary were sitting in their special chairs each banging a wooden spoon on the table. Mary would be having her birthday in a few weeks and he was determined to have enough cash to make the anniversary special.

'Something smells all right, Betty love. What's for tea?'

His wife waved a ladle at him. 'Mutton stew and dumplings followed by a slice of apple pie.'

'I'm sharp-set, love. I'll get washed up and you can serve.' There was no sign of his sister and he was pretty sure she wasn't upstairs as every sound echoed through the house. 'Where's Sarah?'

'She got a message from Mr Hyam to go and see him in Queen Street. It seems there might be some outwork for her after all.'

The boys were in the scullery and burst out drying their hands on their trousers. 'Where's John? We want to tell him what happened with the cat,' Davie said.

'He went with your ma,' Betty told him. 'They should be back any time. Sit down and I'll serve you. Alfie love, you might as well eat and not wait until later.'

'I'll do that. I've got to go out on a bit of business meself so it suits me to eat early.'

She didn't enquire what would be taking him out in the dark and he didn't volunteer an explanation. With luck, and it seemed to be on his side today, he would be out of the house before his sister came back and asked him awkward questions.

12

Sarah was glad she'd brought John with her as she wouldn't have been able to manage to carry the sewing she'd been given to do at home. The payment per item was pitiful, but every penny she earned would be a godsend.

'I'm going to be busy from now on, if I'm going to get all this work done in time, so I want you to look after Mary for me. Can you do that?'

He nodded and almost smiled. 'Good boy. Auntie Betty will be there most of the time but when she has to leave the cottage it will be up to you. You could sing to her – you have a lovely voice.'

To her astonishment and delight he immediately launched into a lively rendering of 'Old King Cole' and when this was done he continued in a like vein with all the nursery rhymes and ditties he had learnt since he was small.

This was a start – with luck he would soon begin to talk as well as sing.

The gaslights made it safe to walk the streets in this part of town, and she wasn't the only woman hurrying about her business in the dark.

Her intention had been to go in by the back gate as always, but Joe had been looking out for her and opened the front door. 'We had a grand time, Ma, and there's a tasty stew for tea and all.'

'You must tell me all about it in a little while, but first I must dispose of these items safely so they won't be mired.'

Her brother called from the kitchen. 'You take the parlour, Sarah love, as your workplace. Put your sewing on the settle and no one will touch it there.'

She could hear Betty upstairs putting the babies to bed, which was kind of her. It might be a squash in this cottage, but both families were settling into a routine, and with her extra bit of income there would be enough for a few luxuries.

Joe had dished up a bowl of stew and Davie was pouring her out a cup of tea. They were good boys; she was sure there weren't many who would do tasks meant for women without complaint.

As she was eating they regaled her with the amusing incident of the cat. Hearing all three of them laugh raised her spirits – even John was smiling by the end of the tale. Bad things happened to good folks and you just had to put your head down and get on with it. If you gave in, things would only get worse.

Alfie was pulling on his boots. 'Are you going to the beer-house?' Sarah asked.

He looked a bit shifty and wouldn't meet her eye. 'I've got a bit of business. I won't be gone long.' He clattered off without saying anything more and she looked at the boys for an explanation.

'He never said nothing to us. I reckon he's going to see Mr Hatch. Right chummy they've become lately,' Joe said as he slurped his tea.

'Needs must. I'm sure your uncle doesn't want to work for him any more than I want to work for Mr Hyam. It's going to be a hard winter, boys, but as long as we stay together we'll get through it.'

Betty tiptoed downstairs and poured herself a well-stewed

mug of tea. 'I'll take care of the house and children, Sarah, so you can work. I know you won't get much, but even a few shillings more will make a difference.'

'Thank you, Betty, that would be a great help. However, I'm intending to do most of the work in the evening. It's not fine stitching – I don't need daylight to do it.'

Joe looked up from the game of marbles he was playing with his brothers. 'What you making then, Ma?'

'I'm not making a whole garment, Joe. My task is to sew the outside seams of the trousers and then I take them back and they go to someone else for the waistband and buttons, and so on to be added. A third person does the finishing – the hems and such.'

The boy scratched his head. She hoped it didn't mean he'd brought nits into the family as they were difficult to get rid of. 'That don't seem sensible to me. What you need is one of them newfangled sewing machines. Have a look, Ma, there's a picture of it in the paper.' He pointed to the well-thumbed copy of the *Essex Standard* that Alfie had been reading before he went out so abruptly.

'Good gracious, what a wonderful invention. Maybe one day I'll be able to afford such a marvel, but until then I must do it the old-fashioned way.'

'When you've finished your tea, Sarah love, I should get on with your sewing. These three are quite big enough to put themselves to bed without waking up the little ones.'

* * *

The oil lamp on the small table beside her was adequate for Sarah to see what she was doing. Although she hadn't been fully trained before she'd left home after her brother Tommy had drowned, she was skilled enough to complete the tasks she had been given. Her fingers flashed in the flickering light and she had completed two items when Betty called softly from the kitchen.

'There's tea here. You've done enough for tonight.'

Sarah was thankful to be called away from this tedious work. Her eyes ached and her fingers also, and the room had become unpleasantly chill. They couldn't afford to have more than the range alight so only the kitchen and the back bedroom were warm.

The overmantel clock, Betty's pride and joy, said it was after ten. Surely her brother should have been back by now?

'Did Alfie say where he was going, Betty?'

'No, meeting a couple of likely customers, I think. Don't know why he's been gone so long – perhaps he's having an ale or two to celebrate a good deal struck.'

'I'm going up. I'm hoping to get another couple of seams finished before the children are awake. The sooner I finish these the quicker I'll be paid. I'd dearly love to be able to put aside a little to buy the children a small gift each at Christmas.'

'I'm making Mary a rag doll for her birthday next month – it would be a shame if we couldn't mark this with a small celebration after so much sadness this year.'

'That's kind of you, Betty. She will appreciate it. Are you waiting up for Alfie?'

'No, the dogs are in the yard so we can go to bed satisfied no one will break in.'

Sarah used the privy, completed her night-time ablutions in the scullery, and took her candle. It was no longer possible to wash in her bedchamber – not only was there no privacy, but by so doing she would disturb the four sleeping children.

She was drifting off to sleep when she heard her friend retire, and slept right through, not even certain her brother had returned at all.

* * *

Hatch was expecting Alfie and beckoned him into his front room and gestured that he take a seat. Considering the bloke was well set up Alfie wondered why he hadn't bought himself a grander drum – moved his wife and children to a bigger house.

'Sit down, Alfie lad. Tell me what you saw.'

'I reckon there's a way in over the back wall that leads to the walk what the night soil men use to empty the privies. I got no notion how many guards there are at night – but there were two at the front and two at the back when I went past yesterday. The padlock is new and will be a bugger to cut through.'

'I've got some here for you to take a squint at. Tell me if you see the one what was on the warehouse door.'

Alfie examined each one carefully. 'This one is the closest. I reckon if you remove the one what's on there and put this one back when you come out, no one will notice the difference until the morning.'

'That's what I thought. Now, you need to get down there again and find out where the guards are stationed and when they take a break for a leak.'

'I'll do that, but I ain't taking no part in the burglary.'

'I've got other men, Alfie lad, to do that. What I need you for is your brains. You see things what I don't see. You're gonna be invaluable to me.'

'I'll not come back to see you again tonight, Mr Hatch. I'll away to my bed when I discover what you need to know. I'll call first thing. I've got a delivery round here.'

It had been several years since he'd had to skulk about in the dark avoiding the eagle eyes of the constables, but he found the ability to merge into the shadows when necessary had not deserted him. He would have felt safer having Buster with him, but his dog was too well known and memorable to risk being seen out at this time of night.

He took the alley that he'd mentioned to Hatch and positioned the orange box he'd brought with him on its end. Using this to stand on he was able to see over the wall without being seen himself.

He stayed there until dawn. At no time was the entrance to the warehouse left unguarded. If one guard left for a call of nature the other remained where he was – ever vigilant. The only way they would affect an entry without being discovered were if he could come up with a disturbance at the front of the building that would draw the guards away without raising their suspicions.

Betty would be beside herself with worry and he had to come up with a reasonable explanation for his absence. He also needed to think of a way Hatch could get his men in and he was too fatigued to do so at the moment.

The dogs greeted him enthusiastically, thinking they might be going for their early morning walk. 'Not now, old fellows, the boys can take you down the river later. I've got to get an hour or two of shut-eye or I'll be fit for nothing today.'

They sloped off, giving him accusing looks over their shoulders as they did so. He was going to get more than a bad look from his wife – that was for sure. He expected his sister would have something to say about his overnight absence as well.

He unlaced his boots and removed them before stepping into the kitchen, then draped his jacket, muffler and hat over the back of the kitchen chair. He crept upstairs like a burglar – well, it was good practice he supposed as he was now a criminal again.

Betty didn't stir as he slid in beside her and he was asleep the instant his head touched the pillow.

* * *

He was woken with a sharp dig in the ribs after what seemed like only a few minutes after he'd got into bed. 'Where were you all night, Alfie Nightingale? Have you got a fancy woman?' This was hissed into his ear and he replied equally quietly.

'Business for Hatch – I'll tell you later. Let me get some sleep, for Gawd's sake.'

'That's all right then. Night, Alfie love.'

She snuggled into him and her warmth was a comfort. He smiled in the darkness. She was satisfied with the answer, had believed him immediately. Funny thing that, six months ago he wouldn't have believed his wife would be so sanguine about him getting up to no good with the likes of Hatch.

The next time he awoke it were to find the bed empty beside him, the cradle also. Bleedin' hell! He'd overslept and he'd yet to come up with a solution to the problem with the guards.

He rolled out of bed, quickly splashed his face in cold water at the washstand, then dragged on his clothes. From the sound of things the entire family was downstairs in the kitchen.

'Morning. You should've woke me, Betty love. I'm right busy this morning and should've been off out already.'

She was feeding pap to Tommy with one hand and stirring porridge with the other. The three boys and Mary was waiting eagerly for their breakfast but there was no sign of his sister. Then he glanced into the front room and saw her industriously sewing by the window. The room was unpleasantly cold and he wished he could light a fire for her.

'If I keep on at this rate, Alfie, I'll have all six pieces done by tomorrow and can ask for a second consignment.'

'Things will get better, Sarah. We've just got to get through this winter.'

'I'm not complaining. Things could be a lot worse. By the way, why were you out so late last night?'

'Met up with a few mates and had a beer or two. Got myself a couple of new customers so it were pennies well spent.' Fortunately, she didn't enquire what these customers wanted as then he would have to have made up further falsehoods.

He just managed to gobble down a plate of porridge and drain his tea before Dickie and Bill turned up eager to get to work. Joe now went with Bill, who was a bit simple, and Davie accompanied Dickie. John, silent as always, remained tied to his ma's skirts.

'Right, you lot, you know what yer doing this morning? Mrs Rawlings, in Wyre Street, is moving into that empty cottage at the end of this road. You'll be doing the shifting for her. Move the small stuff first and then, Joe and Dickie, you can take the big barrow and start bringing the furniture.'

This would keep them occupied all morning and give him time to come up with a solution for Hatch. He was taking a couple of tables and a bench to an alehouse and would need the larger cart first thing.

Then to his surprise John spoke. 'I'll take Buster and Spot down the river for you, Uncle Alfie.'

Betty dropped the porridge pot on the flags and the resulting noise made Mary and his son screech in fright. 'Good lad, that'll be a grand help. You go and put the leashes on. I've just got to lace up me boots.'

The boy dashed off and could be heard quite clearly chattering to the dogs as if it was the most usual thing in the world. Sarah appeared in the kitchen – her smile said it all.

'I can't believe it. After so long, I feared he would never speak again. Will he be all right with those two dogs? He's only six and Buster is twice his size.'

'He will do fine, Sarah love. I'm going most of the way meself. I'll see him into the water meadows, make my deliveries, and then collect him on the way back. Them dogs will take care of him, don't you worry.'

He set off with the child talking non-stop at his side. It were like a stopper pulled from a bottle of beer. His words just came gushing out. 'Right you are, John lad, you go through this gate and let the dogs have a run-around. Maybe they'll catch a plump rabbit for tonight. You stop here until I come back to collect you.'

'I will, and I won't go near the riverbank neither.'

Alfie departed feeling in better spirits than he had for weeks. John back to normal was a good sign. All he had to do now was come up with a plan that would satisfy Hatch and, when the job was done, he would have five guineas in his pocket – with what he got from his barrows this would be more than enough to keep the family until the new year.

* * *

Sarah returned to her sewing, believing that the family had turned a corner. It would take months for her to accept the loss of her beloved Dan, but children were more resilient and they were adjusting to their new, reduced lifestyle and appeared happy enough.

Betty came in holding Mary's hand, and with Tommy on her hip. 'It's too cold for you to stay in here all day, Sarah love, so I'm going to light the fire. Alfie will be getting a lot more in future now he's working for Mr Hatch.'

There was something about this statement that bothered Sarah. 'What sort of work is it that keeps him out all night? Hatch is a villain. Do you think that Alfie has become embroiled in that man's illegal activities?'

Her friend had her back turned whilst she was busy on her knees with the tinderbox and the kindling. Mary staggered over with her arms out. Sarah hastily put her work out of reach of her daughter's fingers and reached down to pick her up.

'You are walking so well, sweetheart, and you are still not quite one year old.' The baby beamed and clapped her hands then waited for Sarah to copy.

Tommy didn't crawl, but was sitting up and trying to stand as well. He was a happy baby and content to lie on his back just kicking his legs in the air – which considering how small the space was in the cottage was a relief to all of them. One baby underfoot was quite sufficient.

'Betty, I won't be satisfied until you've answered me. Is Alfie at risk of being taken up by the constables?'

'Give me a minute to get this blooming fire going and then I'll tell you what I know.'

Once the kindling was burning and the coal arranged on top, Betty sat back wiping her hands on her apron. 'I'll just...'

'No, don't prevaricate. The more you do so, the more worried I become. We both know that he made his fortune from thievery but I'd hoped he'd put that behind him.'

'He never told me about his past, Sarah, and I didn't ask.' Betty stood up, her expression sad. 'I always wondered how he came to be so well set up and him not yet sixteen years of age. I wouldn't have walked out with him if I'd known – I thought he made his money from his carpentry and delivery service.'

'Then I regret having told you. But you must see how worried I am. If he is arrested, then we will all be in the workhouse.'

'We don't get on as well as you and Dan used to. He only married me because I was expecting and then – well you know how things were after little Tommy was born. I'm not going to say anything that will put a rift between us, not when we're getting on so much better.'

'In which case, I'll speak to him when he gets home this

evening. You do understand what this means, Betty? I can't stay here and have my boys dragged into a life of crime. I'm going to write to Mrs Siddons and see if she's still prepared to take us in. There will be little opportunity for them to get into strife in the countryside.'

'If that's what you want, Sarah, then I'll not complain. I think my Alfie has only got involved in this because he's now supporting two families instead of one.'

'I wouldn't be in this mess if he hadn't persuaded Dan to take out a second mortgage and then not paid his share of the repayments. I don't blame him for Dan's death – that was nobody's fault – but...'

'But you think him responsible for you being destitute. You can think again. Your brother told me Dan had got into debt long before Alfie asked him for help. If you hadn't wanted to move to a bigger house, then you wouldn't be in this position. The debts incurred were because of your extravagant tastes.'

Sarah stood up and Mary whimpered. She couldn't speak, her eyes were blurred, and she realised that the cruel words spoken by her friend had a ring of truth. She couldn't stay here a moment longer. She wouldn't wait until she had written a letter and received a reply, but would book a carter and set out immediately for Great Bromley. If she and the children turned up on her grandparents' doorstep they could hardly be rebuffed.

13

Alfie had a brainwave as he was watching the dogs and John playing in the water meadows. The sun was reflected on the water giving it a strange orange light, which reminded him of fire. If one of the blokes started a fire in the building next door to the warehouse the guards would leave their posts and go to help.

Although there were three fire engines in Colchester, supplied by the Essex and Suffolk Insurance Society, the twenty men who worked them would take half an hour at least to arrive at the docks.

The building next door was of a wooden construction and would go up like a candle – the customs warehouse was brick-built, but would still be vulnerable if the wind carried the flames across. Pleased he had come up with a plan, he wished to discuss it with Hatch immediately. When he'd delivered the furniture, and collected his recompense, he headed for his meeting.

He was hoping this would be the end of his involvement but the bastard had other ideas. 'I'll leave you to start the fire, Alfie lad, and then you can scarper. We don't want the constables catching sight of my best man.'

'I ain't starting no fire for you. I told you I wasn't going to do nothing illegal meself.'

'It's up to you, Alfie lad, but if there's men in the building when it goes up and they croak it will be on you.'

He had no option. He couldn't have the deaths of innocent men on his conscience. 'I'll do it – but that's the end of it. I want my five pounds upfront and then I ain't doing nothing more for you. Is that clear?'

Hatch took this information a bit too calmly for his liking. 'Fair enough, you do your bit and I'll do mine.' He tipped five gold coins onto the table and pushed them across to him with a grubby finger. 'Don't say I'm not a man of me word. Here's your payment.'

'When's the job being done?'

'Tonight. You be down there at midnight. When the flames do take hold and you've shouted fire, we'll wait until the guards come to help put it out and then break in.' He slammed his fist down on the table, making Alfie take an involuntary step backwards. 'If things go wrong, it won't be you what suffers, but your family.'

'I gets it, mister, no need for the dramaticals.' Alfie had a bad feeling that it might be harder to break free of Hatch than it had to become involved. He shrugged as if unbothered by the threat. 'I'll not be round again. This is the end of it for me.'

He strode out half-expecting a knife to land between his shoulder blades. No one crossed Hatch and lived to tell the tale. Hadn't he been almost kicked to death himself?

It were time to collect the little 'un and the dogs and get them home. He spied them before he reached the river as they were waiting for him.

'Look what Spot got us, Uncle Alfie.' John held up two fine rabbits with barely a tooth mark on them.

'They will make us a tasty supper and the dogs can have

what's left.' He patted both animals and then ruffled the lad's hair. 'You done well. Your ma will be pleased.'

On the return journey he heard in every detail about the boy's escapade and how the dog had caught two rabbits whilst Buster had been playing in the water.

'That dog's got good sense, John lad. Why should Buster put himself out when Spot can do the work for him?'

He showed John how to clean and skin the coneys out in the yard. Neither Sarah nor Betty would want the mess indoors. 'There, you can give the innards to the dogs and I'll take these in.'

He'd trained Buster to wait until told he could eat, and the younger dog followed his lead. John skipped after him chattering non-stop about nothing in particular. Having longed for weeks to hear the lad's voice, now he was hoping for a bit of peace. The endless rattle was tiring.

'Two rabbits for the pot, Betty love,' he said as he entered.

Her eyes were red and puffy. What was up now? If that bastard had been around threatening his family he would swing for him.

'What's wrong? What's upset you, love?'

'Your Sarah is leaving for Great Bromley. The carter will be here any minute to take them all.' She sniffed. 'She finished the work for Mr Hyam and took it back earlier. The boys have packed their belongings and fetched down the beds and bedding to take with them.'

Sure enough the parlour was filled with Sarah's stuff. She was sitting on the edge of the wooden settle holding Mary. There was no sign of Joe or Davie.

'Why now, Sarah? I thought things was picking up what with your piecework and my...'

'Your what, Alfie? Your illegal activities for Hatch? I can't remain under this roof dreading the knock on the door that would herald the police coming to arrest you. The boys look up to you.

How long would it be before they followed you down the same path?'

She didn't understand that a man had to do whatever it took to keep his family from destitution. 'If it weren't for having you and your brats here I wouldn't have needed to do nothing wrong.' This wasn't what he'd wanted to say but his hurt and anger at her words had taken hold of his tongue.

'Then it's a good thing we're leaving. That's the carter. I wish you, Betty and little Tommy well, but we won't see you again for a while. In fact, not at all until you earn your money honestly again.'

He should have offered to help her load the furniture onto the cart but he was too angry to think straight. 'I got on just fine without you for years. I'll do it again now.'

He turned and fled through the kitchen and out of the small gate that led to the walk. He didn't want to see them go.

* * *

'Ma, the cart's here. Ain't Uncle Alfie going to help?' Joe asked.

'No, son. We will have to manage by ourselves.' There was no expectation of the driver of the cart getting down to assist as he was too old and decrepit to do more than hold the reins of the bony nag.

Then Davie poked his head into the parlour. 'Look who's come a visiting, Ma. It's Mr Billings.'

'Mrs Cooper, Sarah, I can't tell you how sorry I was to hear about Dan. Are you moving away?'

'We're going to live with my grandparents. I would be grateful if you could help us load our things on the cart. Alfie's out somewhere.'

'I'd be happy to. I'll come with you if you like, help you get settled.'

'No, thank you, we will do best on our own.'

Robert didn't enquire why Betty didn't come out to bid them farewell, or why her brother wasn't there either. The boys were eager to leave Colchester and start a new life on a farm. She didn't have the heart to tell them it wasn't going to be a home, that all of them would be little more than servants.

With Robert's assistance everything was piled onto the cart in no time. Then came the tricky problem of removing Spot from his father. He and Buster had bonded and if circumstances were different she might have considered leaving their dog in Colchester.

'Joe, will you go and get the dog? Make sure that Buster doesn't follow you.'

Whilst they were waiting Davie and John scrambled onto the back of the vehicle and then Robert picked her and Mary up and lifted her onto the cart as well.

'This is a bad business, Sarah, and I hope you don't regret your decision. Remember, I'll always stand as your friend.'

He must have guessed she had fallen out with Alfie, and probably knew why. 'Thank you, Robert, I shan't forget your kindness. I know it won't be an ideal arrangement, that all of us will have to work for our keep, but the boys will be away from temptation and that's what matters. I was curious as to why my brother took the boys for a picnic the other week – now I'm certain it's because he needed them with him to further his criminal activities.'

There was no further opportunity for private conversation as Joe returned with their dog. 'There ain't room for him on the cart with us; he'll have to run alongside. I've got him on his lead, Ma.'

'Good boy, I knew I could rely on you to do the sensible thing. Is Buster securely confined in the yard?'

'He ain't there. Uncle Alfie must have taken him out with him.'

Joe hopped nimbly onto the cart to join her brothers while still hanging on to the rope. She shook hands with Robert and then shifted as far back on the cart as she could to avoid being cata-pulted onto the cobbles. The ride would be smoother once they left Colchester and were travelling on hardpacked dirt rather than knobbly cobbles.

The dog trotted happily beside them making no attempt to slip his lead and run off. When they were safely away from the town and trundling towards Clingoe Hill, she thought it safe for the dog to be released.

'He won't run away now, Ma; he'll want to stay with us,' Joe said as he slipped the rope from the dog's neck.

'He will probably disappear occasionally to explore the fields and woods we pass, but I'm sure he won't let us get too far ahead of him.'

The cart rocked to a standstill. 'Orf you get, missus. We won't get up this hill otherwise.'

Sarah handed the baby to Joe and then jumped down. Davie helped his little brother and then she collected Mary and Joe joined them at the side of the road.

'Look, Ma, we ain't the only ones on foot,' Davie pointed out.

'It makes sense to not put too much strain on that poor horse. We want him to convey us and our belongings another few miles and then he has to return all the way back to his stable.'

The dog was delighted to have them next to him and the brisk walk up the long hill was quite enjoyable after being bumped and jolted for over an hour on the back of the ancient cart.

By the time they were approaching Great Bromley the novelty of the journey had worn thin. Mary was asleep, but John was constantly demanding to know when they would arrive at their

new home. Joe and Davie had long since got down and were
larking about in the fields with the dog.

'I'm not sure of the exact direction of Hockley Farm, but I'm
sure there will be no difficulty discovering its whereabouts.'

The carter grunted but made no further response. They had
turned off the main thoroughfare that led to Clacton-on-Sea some
time ago and were now travelling along a narrow lane bordered
by high hawthorn hedges. She hadn't seen or heard the boys for
some time and was concerned they might have become lost after
the cart had turned.

Then John, who was standing up hanging on to the furniture
in order to get a better look, began to wave. 'I see them, Ma –
they're just ahead. I think they've found where we're supposed
to be.'

She climbed down from the cart and, with Mary in her arms
and John hanging on to her skirt, she hurried to join the boys.
Presumably their belongings would follow behind. The sun was
setting, and there was a distinct nip in the air heralding cold
weather to come. She was glad she had made the decision now as
making the journey when the weather was inclement would have
been far more unpleasant.

Joe wasn't looking happy; in fact he was looking decidedly
miserable. 'This is it, Ma, but it ain't what I expected. I don't
reckon there will be room for all of us if that's the farmhouse
down the end of the lane.'

She looked where he pointed and her heart sunk to her boots.
All she could see was an ancient cottage with a sagging roof and
dirty windowpanes. Had she made the most dreadful error in
bringing her family here?

The sound of the cart approaching behind them meant they
had to make a move. She couldn't stand here dithering – whatever

circumstances she had brought them to she had no choice but to endure.

John tugged at her hand. 'There's no smoke coming from the chimney, Ma. I don't think no one lives there.'

'In which case, that can't be the farmhouse. It must be further ahead. We've made excellent time, and should be able to settle ourselves before it gets dark.' She prayed her words would not prove to be false hope, that her unpleasant grandmother would not reject them.

* * *

Alfie regretted his outburst but thought it best to remain absent until Sarah, Mary and the boys had gone. Buster seemed to sense there was something wrong and instead of rushing about in the water meadows he remained at his side, whining occasionally and pressing his cold nose into Alfie's palm.

'I know, old fellow, things ain't right now – but Sarah will be better off away from here. I wish I could run off, go back to London and work with George Benson again.' Things had been simple then, only himself and Buster to worry about. Now it were too complicated and he were weighed down by his responsibilities.

His sister would have been better off if he'd stayed away from her. He were bad news – that's for sure. First it had been his fault their little brother Tommy had drowned in this very river four years past; next his best friend Jim had died and he should've taken better care of him. Then he got Betty into trouble and she'd been ill after the baby had been born and now he'd ruined his sister's life by getting Dan into debt.

He was tempted to head for the station and take the train back to Town, but he couldn't leave his wife and child to the mercy of that bastard Hatch. He had no choice but to accept he were no better than the villain himself, and get on with his life as best he could.

Buster sniffed around the yard and in the workshop looking for Spot. 'They've gone. We've got to get on without them. I reckon you can sleep indoors again if you want.'

The dog cocked his ear as if he understood the words but when Alfie pointed up the steps to the back door the dog turned his back and walked into the workroom and flopped down on the sacks he'd shared until today.

'Suit yourself. Betty will be pleased you want to stay out here.'

The cottage seemed empty, but there was stew bubbling on the range and his wife greeted him with a smile.

'It won't be the same, Alfie love, but we'll manage together. I know we parted on bad terms with Sarah, but she'll be in touch in a few weeks and maybe we can go out and see her in the spring.'

'I don't want to talk about it – not now. What's for tea? Smells good.' He reached down and picked up the baby who was gurgling and waving his arms, eager to be reunited with his pa. He dandled his son on his knee and was reluctant to put him down when Betty placed the plate in front of him.

'Here, I'll take him. You get on with your meal, Alfie. I'll get this little man to bed.'

However upset he were, he never lost his appetite – he thought this was because he'd spent all that time in London half-starved. He wasn't sure what he was going to tell Betty about tonight's business. Better she didn't know the truth just in case the constable came making enquiries.

Little Tommy settled into his cradle without a murmur and she was downstairs again as he scraped the last of the tasty stew off his plate. 'That were tasty, Betty love. Is there any more?'

'No point in keeping it – not enough to make another meal tomorrow.'

They sat companionably, she drinking tea, he finishing off his second plate of stew. 'I'm off out again in a bit, Betty love. A bit of business for Hatch – you know how it is.'

'I know you wouldn't be involved with him if it wasn't for us. Sometimes good men have to do bad things and I won't think any the worse of you. Just promise me you won't hurt anyone. I couldn't forgive you if you did that.'

Alfie shuddered. If he weren't careful tonight there could be casualties. If the fire took hold before the fire engines arrived then God knows what might happen.

He read yesterday's paper whilst she got on with some mending. She was unusually quiet, normally after a few moments silence she began chattering again – not tonight. Possibly like him she was mulling over how their lives had changed over the past few months.

'Here, Betty love, you take this. Put it somewhere safe.' He dropped the five golden coins onto the table and he expected her to exclaim, to pick one up to examine it, to show some sort of pleasure – but she did not react in any way.

The coins spun, the light from the oil lamp making them glitter, and then all five of them rested in the centre of the table. Why didn't she look at him? Then she raised her head and the look she gave him was like a blow to the chest.

'Dear God, what are you going to have to do tonight in order to earn so much? I don't want this. It's blood money and I'd rather go to the poorhouse than use it.' She pushed herself upright, scattering the mending unheeded to the floor. 'Sarah was right to leave. If I could do the same, Alfie Nightingale, then I would go too.'

'Don't be bloody stupid, woman. Cash is cash and it don't

matter where it came from. Tomorrow I'll go to the bank and put the deeds of this cottage in your name, then I'll take out the few pounds we still have left and give it to you.' He scooped up the coins and dropped them back into his pocket.

'You don't have to use this – I'll need it when I leave here tomorrow. You can take in a couple of lodgers, sell this place for all I care.'

'That's right, run away again like you did last time. You're not man enough to stay and put things right. You're not the man I thought you were, Alfie Nightingale, and Tommy and I will do very well without you.'

She stormed off upstairs leaving him to contemplate the disaster his life had become. She didn't understand he had been trapped by Hatch into doing this job for him, and he wasn't going to bother to explain it. It weren't her place to question the master of the house – she would do what he bloody well told her or suffer the consequences.

He put the coins in an empty pot in the scullery. No point in taking them with him and risking losing them. Although he said he was leaving, were going to give her his house, he'd changed his mind. Too bad she didn't like the man he'd become. He weren't too keen on her neither; they just had to make the best of it like everyone else.

He should've told her this was to be the only thing he intended to do for Hatch, that from now on he would make his money legitimately, but too late now. The damage was done. A few months ago he'd been on top of the world. His business had been growing, he was making good money from his carpentry and his sister was married to Dan and living the sort of life she could only have dreamed of a couple of years ago.

Now she was a widow, the boys were orphans, and she was

forced to go and live with the people who had rejected their own ma, and all because of him.

Sarah saw there were half a dozen pigs rootling around in the
field to the left of the drive. She could hear cattle lowing mourn-
fully somewhere ahead, so this farm had livestock as well as
growing crops. The farm looked prosperous. They walked past the
dilapidated cottage and saw it was unoccupied – which was a
relief.

When they turned the bend in the drive, they saw a range of
buildings and the farmhouse just ahead. There were well-fed
chickens and ducks foraging for grain whilst a miserable farm cat
sat watching them from a wall. 'Hang on to Spot, Joe. We don't
want him chasing that cat.'

'Righto, Ma, I'll not let go of him,' the boy replied.

The cart was still a distance behind them as the horse was
now tired, which made progress slow.

'Davie, please go and knock on the door. Remember, children,
Mr and Mrs Siddons are not aware that we are arriving to live with
them and might not be as happy as we are about the situation.'

She shook the worst of the dust from her skirts, adjusted her bonnet, and followed the boy to the door. There was no knocker to use so he banged with his fist. Joe had the sense to stand behind her with the dog so Spot wouldn't at first be visible.

After a few moments the door creaked open and a stick-thin, grey-haired gentleman stood there. He stared at them in bewilderment for a few seconds and then his eyes brightened and he smiled.

'You must be Sarah – you've come to live with us after all.' He stepped aside and was about to invite them in when her grandmother appeared behind him.

'Well then, what have we here? Don't think you're bringing someone else's brats into my house, Sarah. You and the baby can come in, but those three and that dog can find themselves somewhere in the barn to sleep.'

'They are my children, ma'am, and I won't be parted from them.'

The woman, her eyes snapping and her thin lips set in a harsh line, was about to slam the door in their face when her grandfather intervened.

'Now, Elsie love, there's no need to be hasty. Why don't they move into the cottage? They will all be together then and not getting under your feet.'

'Very well, Jethro, if you insist. I'll expect to see all of you here at five o'clock Monday morning. You don't get breakfast until you've worked for it.'

The door closed leaving them standing in the cold with no prospect of a hot meal or anywhere warm and dry to live. She gathered her wits and stiffened her spine. If she gave in then what would become of her children?

'Quickly, Joe, run back and get the cart to stop outside the cottage. I know it's a dismal place, but it's better than sleeping in a barn. I'm sure once we have proved our worth my grandmother will relent towards us and things will improve.'

Mary was beginning to grizzle and she could feel the wet from the baby's napkin seeping into the front of her shawl. From the smell the baby had emptied her bowels as well as her bladder. Davie ran ahead with his brother but John clung to her hand like a drowning man.

They hadn't been given the key so she must presume the cottage was unlocked. Thank God she had had the foresight to bring an oil lamp, candles and a flint with her. Also, she had packed sufficient food to last them for the next day or two.

Joe already had the door open and was starting to unload the cart. She hadn't expected to be obliged to do this job on her own but had no option if they were to get everything inside before it was too dark to see what they were about.

In the end they had to prop the beds against the wall as the carter insisted he had to leave if he was to return to Colchester before it got dark. He had already been well recompensed for his trouble, so Sarah turned her back on him and let him go about his business without a qualm.

'Joe, you and Davie will have to bring in everything else. I must change Mary and begin to put things away. It will be unpleasant here for a day or two but I promise I'll make this into a home as soon as may be.'

Joe spoke up. 'It ain't much, Ma, but it's better than being in the farmhouse with them if they don't want us. Here we're together like what we should be. I saw some men in the fields – so they don't really need us to work for them, do they?'

'You could be right, Joe, but Mrs Siddons did come and see me and say we could live with them in return for our labour. I don't know much about life on a farm, but I'm fairly sure workers are entitled to a hot meal before they return to their homes. Which means we will be well fed at least.'

'I reckon she don't want to pay them so wants us to do the work for nothing. Them two old folk couldn't take care of the live-stock and everything else without help,' Joe said knowledgeably. 'I'm looking forward to learning about farming, Ma. Me and Davie will soon pick it up and make ourselves useful.'

'The barns and such were well repaired, Ma. It's just this place what's falling down,' Davie said cheerfully.

The cottage was gloomy because of the filthy windows. There was a kitchen and scullery at the back. It had no modern range, but an iron grate with two trivets; she had managed with less than this before so would make it work. Apart from one other room, too derelict to use, this was all there was on the ground floor.

'Come along, sweetheart, let me get you clean and dry again.' Sarah spread out the already damp and smelly shawl on top of the filthy kitchen table and placed her precious daughter on top. As soon as Mary was comfortable she stopped crying and was chuckling and laughing and eager to be put down on the floor to explore.

'No, you can't do that, not until I've scrubbed everywhere. You're far too fond of putting things in your mouth and I shudder to think what you might find in here.'

Despite the protests of her daughter she refashioned the shawl into a carrier and tied the child back in position. However, this time she put her facing front so she could see what was going on.

By the time the boys had dragged the beds upstairs it was full dark. There were only two bedchambers, neither large as they were under the eaves of the roof. 'You can just about fit your beds in here, Joe, and Mary and I will take the other room.'

Sarah wasn't looking forward to sleeping on the boards with only a thin straw-filled mattress between her and the rodents that infested the place.

'Davie, go with your brother and find that half-starved cat. We'll make it ours, then it can clear the house of mice for us.'

'Won't Spot try and eat it?'

'No, son, not when he knows the cat's part of the family. Where is the dog? I've not seen him since we moved in.'

Joe looked up from hammering in the pegs that held the bed together. 'He's having an explore. He knows where we are and he'll be back soon enough.'

* * *

Some instinct for survival made Alfie decide to leave his home through the small gate in the back wall that led to the walk that the night soil men used. If anyone made enquiries he could deny having left his house and no one would be able to prove different.

He'd got the tinderbox, a couple of candle ends and some slivers of dry wood in his deep pockets and he hoped this would be enough to start the fire in the building next door to the warehouse. He also had a couple of necessary tools in his other pocket.

He kept to the shadows, took a circuitous route to the docks and was sure no one had seen him. He had his cap pulled down over his ears and his muffler obscured the lower half of his face. With his collar turned up as well he doubted even his own ma would recognise him. Despite the dire circumstances his mouth curved. Ma wouldn't recognise him in his birthday suit as the last time she'd seen him he'd been a boy; now he was taller than most men and had a fine set of whiskers.

The building that stood no more than a yard or two from the warehouse, which Hatch intended to rob, was used as a store by the wheelwright next door. There shouldn't be anyone inside at this time of night, but he'd make sure before he set it on fire.

The man what owned this building would be sadly out of pocket by his hand, and this bothered him. It made him even more determined he would never become embroiled in that bastard's schemes again. If it meant selling up and moving somewhere else with his family, then that was what he would do.

He edged his way towards the building and then froze. Someone was there – he definitely heard men speaking. His heart hammered in his chest. His mouth was dry and his hands clammy. He leant against the wall and took several deep breaths, trying to calm his agitation. It wouldn't do no one any good if he lost his nerve and failed to complete his task.

As he calmed he realised the coves were the guards outside the warehouse – they wasn't anywhere near him. Sound carried more at night – he should have remembered that. The storehouse was, as expected, unoccupied, and Alfie crept in. He'd heard more than one church clock strike the hour – his task was to have the fire burning and the guards distracted at midnight, which gave him about half an hour.

The padlock on this building was easy to prise off and he pulled the doors closed behind him. As long as no night-watchman came to check he should be safe enough. The fire needed to be well alight before he left so he'd better get on with it. His intention was to set the blaze and then nail the padlock back in place when he was outside. With luck, no one would ever discover the fire had been set deliberately.

He struck the flint and blew on the fluff in the tinderbox and it caught immediately. From this he lit the candle ends. He'd already put the slivers of dry wood underneath a pile of loose timber and other debris. Although there were holes in the roof, this pile of stuff was dry enough to catch quickly – at least he hoped it was.

He carefully put the candle ends in with the kindling and stood back waiting to see if this worked. For a minute or two there was little to see or hear and then the flames took hold and he staggered backwards to avoid being burnt. He ran headlong for the door, barely had time to get out and replace the padlock before the fire took a real hold. The sound of the flames was terrifying – like a beast roaring in pain.

He ran into the shadows and then shouted the alarm. Immediately the cry was taken up and the sound of pounding boots approaching meant he had to leg it before he was discovered. His part was done – it was up to Hatch and his men to do the rest.

He was halfway home when the fire engines, drawn by stout horses, galloped by. He needed to get home and remove his outer garments, these smelled of smoke and would give away his reason for being out so late if he was apprehended.

He saw no one and heard nothing untoward and was sure he had completed his side of the bargain without the risk of being brought to justice. Buster was waiting by the gate to greet him.

'Hush, old fellow, I'm back now. Are you coming inside?'

This time his dog accompanied him into the kitchen and flopped down in front of the still-warm range with a sigh of what sounded like contentment. Alfie quickly stripped off his outer garments and hung them in the scullery. Then he scrubbed himself down, removing the last trace of any evidence that he had been the one to cause the conflagration at the docks.

He didn't want to sleep beside Betty, so found himself a blanket, made a pillow from his clothes, and curled up in front of the range with his dog.

* * *

The cottage was little more than a hovel. There were tiles missing on the roof and everywhere was damp. Wind whistled in through the gaps in the window frames and neither the front nor back door fitted snugly enough to prevent draughts. This was no place for young children to live and Sarah feared for the health of her daughter if they were obliged to remain in this dismal place for long.

She'd done her best to clean the kitchen so it was habitable, but even with the fire going the room was cold and miserable, as were the children and herself.

'I know things look bleak, my dears, but somehow we will make this place more comfortable. Joe has the tools that your uncle gave him, and a bag of nails. I'm sure we can find something to repair the holes in the windows and the walls.'

The boys were sitting silently around the table; only the baby remained cheerful. She was in her special chair and happily banging a wooden spoon on the table and laughing at the noise.

'We should have stopped in Colchester. At least we would have been warm and welcome there,' Joe said.

'We are here now, son, and must make the best of it. Eat your stew and finish up the bread as I have no wish to encourage the mice.'

The dog had not yet returned and she was becoming concerned, but didn't like to draw attention to his absence as the boys had more than enough to be despondent about. The cat was in the scullery awaiting her attention.

'I'm going to try and comb out the fleas from the cat – then he will need a bath. Does anyone wish to help me with this unpleasant task? He cannot come into the house until he's vermin-free.'

All three perked up at the suggestion and were eager to assist. She got them each to cut holes for their arms and head in a sack and then pull them on like a jerkin. She hoped her apron would be sufficient to protect her from the fleas.

'Now, boys, do you have your piece of soap? Make sure it is sufficiently wet to trap the flea when you bang it down upon it.'

The kitchen was so filthy, the table as bad, that she thought it would make no discernible difference adding fleas and dirt to what was already there. She was fairly sure there would be no resident fleas or bugs as the cottage had been empty, possibly for years, and they would have had nothing to feed on.

She picked the cat up in a sack and it purred. The noise so loud it filled the scullery and the boys laughed.

'Cor, listen to that. I never heard a cat sound so happy. What are we going to call him, Ma?' Davie asked.

'It's impossible to tell the colour of his fur as it is so matted and dirty. Once he is clean we might find it easier to name him. After all, Spot is named after his appearance.'

'Why isn't he back yet? Can I go and call him, Ma?'

'As soon as we've finished with the cat you can go and look for him, Davie. I think it would be best if we got this over with before we brought the dog into the house. I have a feeling that it might take time for the two of them to become friends.'

She had brought with her two tin baths, one large enough for her and the boys to complete their ablutions and a smaller one for the baby. This was placed on a sack, the last one they owned, in the centre of the table. The rest of the surface was covered with newspaper.

'Cats as a rule object to being in water, so I expect we shall all be scratched and possibly bitten before this procedure is completed.'

John was kneeling on a chair. 'The water's warm. I reckon he'll like it.'

She was certain he would not and was correct in her

assumption. From purring and placid the feline was transformed into a wriggling, spitting, scratching beast. It took all four of them to wash the dirt from his fur, comb him to remove the majority of his fleas, and then wrap him in a rag to dry him off.

John and Davie continued to slam down their pieces of soap on any remaining fleas. 'We've got hundreds, Ma,' John said. 'Do you want us to scrape them off so we can use the soap ourselves?'

'No, now we've finished wrap everything, including the sack, in the newspaper and put it on the fire.'

As they were no longer tormenting him, the cat stopped struggling and began to purr again. She handed the clean, dry animal to Joe. 'He's a handsome fellow. His grey and white will be a perfect match for Spot.'

'Let's call him Smoke – I never seen the like. After what we've done to him, he's purring again.'

'What do you think, boys?'

The consensus was that Smoke suited the new addition to the family perfectly. She'd kept back the scrapings from the stewpot and put this in a chipped saucer. The cat gobbled it down and then curled up in front of the fire to lick himself dry.

'I'm going to put your sister to bed, boys, whilst you go and find the dog. Make sure you have him on the lead when you bring him in as I don't want him to chase Smoke.'

They removed the sacks on the way and hung them on nails against the wall outside. Hopefully any unpleasant visitors would die or hop away during the night. Mary was so sleepy she didn't protest at being put to bed in a strange place. John had insisted the baby remained at the end of his bed, and she was relieved he had been prepared to keep Mary with him.

The chamber she had chosen for the children was directly above the kitchen and the chimney breast ran through the room, making it less chill than the room she was to occupy. Fortunately, the missing tiles were on her side of the cottage, not theirs.

There was no need for her to sing a lullaby as the baby was asleep before her head touched the bed. Sarah picked her way down the creaking staircase, expecting at any moment to be pitched forward as the wood disintegrated beneath her boots.

The parlour was uninhabitable. The walls had holes in them and there appeared to be a flock of birds nesting in the chimney. This door would be kept closed and they would be obliged to live entirely in the kitchen.

The cat stood up and with its tail standing up walked towards her, eager to be fussed. Just as she was about to stoop down and pick it up the back door screeched open and the boys and the missing dog blundered in.

Smoke arched his back. Spot froze. She was about to intervene when something quite extraordinary occurred. The cat sauntered over and rubbed himself, still purring loudly, against the dog.

Spot lowered his head and gave the cat a lick. Her breath hissed through her teeth. 'Good heavens! I do believe they are going to be the best of friends.'

Joe released his hold on the dog and held up what he had in his other hand. 'Look at this, Ma, Spot's brought us back our supper for tomorrow.'

'Put the rabbits in the scullery. I'll attend to them before I go up.'

'I'm the man of the house now, Ma. I'll do it.' Joe squared his shoulders and stared at her. With his mop of black curls, bright blue eyes and even features he was so like his father it was hard to deny him anything.

'You are indeed, young man, and I shall rely on you to keep this family together. It's Sunday tomorrow. I doubt there's a church within walking distance, so we will spend the day doing what we can to improve this cottage. Once you boys go to the farmhouse your time will not be yours and you will be working long hours outside in the fields.'

'That won't be so bad – I want to learn to be a farmer,' Joe said. 'I reckon Davie and me could look after the pigs and John can take care of the birds.'

15

Alfie was woken by the sound of his son crying and then Betty getting up to take care of him. He sat up bleary-eyed, yawned and scrambled to his feet. He riddled the range and got it going again and then filled the basin with hot water and fetched his razor and strap from the scullery. He had just completed shaving when his wife arrived with Tommy in her arms.

She didn't greet him with her usual friendly smile but planted the baby in his chair and busied herself making tea. He needed to put things right between them as he couldn't live in this atmosphere and he'd not changed his mind about leaving his family.

'Betty love, I'm that sorry for saying what I did last night. You're a good wife to me and I would be lost without you – especially now Sarah's gone.'

Mentioning his sister was a mistake. 'You would prefer to live with her rather than with your lawful wife, wouldn't you? It's always Sarah first with you.'

This was going to be harder than he thought. 'We've always been close, Sarah and me, and having been apart for so long it's made us even closer. She wouldn't have had to go and live with her grandparents if it hadn't been for me. Getting my hand stamped on by Hatch's minions wouldn't have happened if I'd not riled the man. I should have had more sense than to ever get mixed up with him.'

He had been talking to her back, but her shoulders were no longer as rigid as before. 'There's no use thinking like that, Alfie love. What's done is done. Always better to bend than break, is what my ma used to say.'

'Sit down, love. I think I need to be straight with you. Tell you what I had to do last night, and why.'

She wasn't as shocked as he'd expected when he finished his story. 'As long as no one was murdered, and you didn't actually steal anything, I understand. Do you really think that man will harm us if you don't do as he bids?'

'I think he'll leave us alone for a bit; he got what he wanted. But I reckon he'll be back when he's got another job planned and wants me to be involved. I'm not doing anything else illegal like. I thought I would sell the cottage and we could move away and start again.'

'If he hears the cottage is for sale, he'll know you're planning to leave. And what about Sarah? I know how upset she was when she discovered your ma had gone off without saying where she'd gone – surely you don't want to do that to her again?'

'I'll do whatever I need to, to keep you and little Tommy safe. And it's different – I'll write to her when we're settled so she knows where we are.'

'Are you thinking of going back to London?'

'No, I thought we could go to Chelmsford. Now there's trains every day, we can be there in an hour. It ain't as big as Colchester, but there will be something there for us, don't you fret.'

'Why don't we go there for a day out first? We've got the

money from last night and can use that to rent somewhere with a yard and workroom. Your hand is almost better...'

'It won't ever be right. I'll never be able to make cabinets and suchlike again. I reckon I can make the baby chairs, benches, tables and things what don't require me to use the hand too much. I think I might know someone who will buy the cottage and contents as well as my tools and barrows.'

Her expression changed and her eyes filled. She now understood the enormity of the situation – that in order to get away safely they would have to abandon everything she treasured. It was too far and too slow to employ a carter to take her precious china, crockery and furniture to Chelmsford. They would have to go to the station as if having a day out or someone would inform that bastard and he would stop them leaving.

'I can't leave my wedding gifts – the beautiful furniture you made us, my rocking chair...'

'We've got to leave everything, Betty love, even our garments. There'll be more than enough rhino to buy it all again.'

The church bells were clanging, demanding that all who heard them take themselves in their Sunday best to worship. The likes of him and Betty were obliged to stand at the back. It was the grand folk sat in the pews.

'I've got to take Buster out for his constitutional, Betty love. Why don't you come with us?'

'No thank you, it's too damp and cold to take the baby out unless it's essential. I'll spend the time sorting out any valuables we can take. I thought that I could wear several petticoats and drawers and two gowns, then at least I'd have something to change into when we go.'

'A good idea. I think I could do the same. I've still got me big coat from when I came down from London. It's got plenty of pockets to put small things in.' She'd taken his suggestion that they move as soon as possible without too much fuss.

'I'll be an hour or so, love. I'll wander around to see the gent what has been showing an interest in me business. He ain't no friend of Hatch so won't snitch on me.'

It were nippy out so he put on his heavy overcoat, the one what he'd been talking to Betty about, not the one he'd worn last night, and headed for the river. Now he'd made the decision to scarper he were eager to set things in motion, remove his wife and son from danger.

His thoughts turned to his sister and her hasty departure yesterday. He was glad she had gone; she would be safer with their grandparents, however reluctant they might be to accommodate her and the boys. Once he was settled he'd send for her. This weren't going to happen for a few months, but in the spring things might be different.

The cove he wanted to see were a sailor what had made his fortune in some far-off place and had returned to his home town wanting to set up his own business and find himself a wife. He were lodging down by the station and weren't likely to be at church neither.

He crossed the river and reminded the dog to stay at his heel. It might be the Lord's day, but there were plenty of vehicles trundling up and down North Station Road. The talk went better than he'd dreamed of. The deal was struck and the money and deeds could be exchanged when the bank opened the next day.

Betty's notion that they visit Chelmsford first in order to find somewhere to live were too risky. Someone would tell Hatch they'd gone out and he would be waiting on their doorstep when they returned, and they might never get the chance to leave again.

He bought tickets for himself, Betty, and the dog to travel the next morning. This time he weren't going to sit in the third-class compartments, them that were open to the elements, but in second class along with the other business gents.

Betty had been busy in his absence and the cottage was sparkling. There were tasty pasties waiting for his midday meal and even a jug of beer to wash it down.

'It's done, Betty love. We're off tomorrow. I've just to meet the purchaser at the bank where he'll exchange the money for the deeds. I got an excellent price. Seventy-five pounds is a fortune and we'll find something grand to rent. I reckon we might find ourselves a smart house what's fully furnished, if I'm prepared to pay a bit extra.'

'This will be our last night in this house, Alfie love. Are you going to share my bed tonight?'

'Of course I am. I ain't sleeping on the floor again if I can help it.'

Inevitably in the cosy warmth of the marital bed one thing led to another and they shared more than were sensible in the circumstances. The last thing he wanted was another mouth to feed especially as Betty might well be unable to cope after, and be poorly, like what she was with Tommy.

* * *

Sarah was awakened by the sound of water dripping onto the floorboards by the window. She was stiff and cold but at least the rain hadn't come in directly above the mattress. She lay for a few moments listening to it hammering on the tiles. There was no light filtering in through the filthy panes so it couldn't be later than six o'clock – possibly a lot earlier.

She sat up and found the tinderbox she'd placed beside her on the floor. As soon as she had a candle lit she hastily got dressed. Under normal circumstances no one wore their outside boots in the house but the cottage was too cold and damp for padding about in stockings or bare feet.

She paused outside the other room and could hear the children breathing softly. The longer they stayed asleep the better. It would give her more time to at least clean the kitchen so it would be safe for Mary to totter about.

The stairs creaked ominously but she reached the bottom without putting her foot through the rotten treads. The kitchen was marginally warmer as the remains of the fire still glowed in the grate. Thank God she had taken a sack of coal with her. They would freeze without it. Little point in sending the boys out to forage for burnable timber when everything would be saturated after the deluge that had been pouring down all night.

Spot was waiting by the back door and at first she didn't see the cat. 'My word, you are certainly good friends if you both wish to go out in the rain together.'

The dog thumped his tail and the cat wound itself in and out of his legs, purring loudly. The back door didn't budge at first and she had to apply her shoulder to it before it opened. The animals vanished into the blackness unperturbed by the inclement weather. She pulled the door shut before the howling gale blew out the candle.

The only good thing about this hovel was the fact that she would hear through the kitchen ceiling when Mary woke up. John had taken to putting the baby on the chamber pot as soon as she woke, which meant only the occasional wet draw sheet to launder.

Water had to be fetched from the well she'd seen in the backyard. She had no option but to collect two buckets and brave the elements as she couldn't get on with the necessary cleaning without water.

Something soft squished beneath her boot as she stepped into the scullery. She bit back her squeal and backed out to collect the oil lamp. She assumed the cat wasn't used to being inside and had left her an unpleasant reminder.

Her mouth widened when she saw what she had trodden on. It was a dead mouse – and there were a dozen more of them side by side on the floor. Smoke was already earning his place in the family. She took a brush in order to sweep them up. As she was doing so she realised there were half a dozen tails and a dozen ears amongst the bodies. The cat had had his breakfast already.

After an hour and a half of back-breaking scrubbing she sat back on her heels and surveyed the flagstones. They were cracked and pitted from long use, but now they were clean and the whole room smelt fresher. All she had to do now was clean the windows with some vinegar and newspaper. The room was definitely lighter when she'd finished.

The fire was hot enough to put the kettle on and the dough she'd set to rise last night was ready to knock back and put in the bread oven built into the wall beside the fireplace. The rabbits had already been skinned and cleaned by Joe and he'd made a remarkably good job of it. She deftly dismembered both corpses and dropped them into the pan along with two onions, three potatoes and some turnips. This would cook slowly all day and make a delicious tea for them all, and should do for two further meals. She'd brought the old saucepan she had used to cook the vegetable peelings for the chickens and decided she would do this today. She thought she might have heard at least one bird roosting in a building across the yard.

There was no handsome dresser upon which to put her crockery and precious clock. All she had now were a couple of rickety shelves that she didn't trust to support the weight without collapsing. This was the first task she would ask Joe to attend to.

She prayed that he'd worked often enough with his uncle to be able to mend these shelves.

There was no milk and she had no intention of going to the farmhouse to ask for any, not today. The porridge would have to be made with water this morning and the children would have to learn that, however unpalatable, everything that was set before them must be eaten.

Today they would have jam with their bread, but in future it would be kept for special occasions. A loud bark outside the door heralded the arrival of the animals. They couldn't come in until she'd found two relatively dry sacks and given them both a thorough rub. Only then would she allow them to mar her pristine flagstones.

Spot stood obediently whilst she raised each of his paws, wiped them, and then allowed her to dry his shaggy coat. Smoke was already in front of the fire and didn't object when she picked him up and gave him a similar treatment.

'There you are – you can stay in now. I can hear the children waking and must go up to collect Mary. Spot, you stay here. Smoke you must come with me and start catching the mice in the roof.'

When she reached the bottom of the staircase Joe appeared, his hair over his eyes, but with an unexpected grin. 'We could hear you talking to the animals, Ma, as if they can understand.'

She put her hands on her hips and pursed her lips. 'Well, young man, as the dog has remained where I told him to and the cat is at this very moment walking up the stairs I rather think they can.'

He laughed, and she joined in. John appeared with Mary in his arms.

'Here you are, Ma, she's a good girl and all clean and dry this morning.'

Sarah collected her daughter and gave John a quick hug. 'I don't know what I'd do without you boys – you are making a dreadful situation so much easier. Put on your warmest clothes. I fear we are all going to have to venture outside at some point.'

'Your hair's wet, Ma. Have you already been out to collect the water?' Joe's tone was almost accusatory.

'I have, son, but in future I shall leave you and Davie to do the heavy work. You'll see why I had to go myself when you come down.'

Over breakfast she told them about the mice and they were suitably impressed. The rain slackened halfway through the morning and the older boys rushed off with all four buckets to fill them at the well.

'John, do you think you could take care of Mary for a while whilst I go out and see if there's anything of use in the sheds out there?'

'Course I can. She's no trouble at all. We'll play with the spoons until you get back, Ma.'

With her shawl tied tightly around her shoulders and her skirts hitched up and tucked into her petticoat to keep them from the mud, she went to investigate her new domain.

'There's a couple of chickens living in that shed, Ma; maybe we'll find an egg or two.' Davie pointed to the nearest building, the one with the least sagging roof and the most tiles still in place. She'd been right, as when she peered through the empty window frame, there were not just two chickens, but a clutch of chicks as well. These couldn't fly in and out of the window like their mother so the boys hadn't realised they were there.

'I'm going to fetch some crusts and a handful of grain to give them. With luck, we can keep these here and Mrs Siddons will be none the wiser.'

She took a chipped basin full of water and a bowl with the

cooked vegetable peelings to the shed and carefully opened the door. The chicks tried to hide under their mother's wings but the hens knew that the arrival of a human carrying a bowl meant food. If they hadn't moved into the cottage the chicks would have died as there was no food for them in here.

She put the water bowl down and tipped the contents of the other onto the dirt. The two skinny hens dived head first into the food. The little ones, seeing the adults eating, followed suit. The boys arrived at her side, drawn by the noise.

'Look at that – we've got our own little flock. I bet they'll be some cocks amongst that lot and they make fine eating when they're fattened up,' Joe said.

Davie put down the full bucket of water and began to search amongst the debris in the shed and found the hollow with half a dozen eggs in it. 'I reckon these are fresh, Ma; they smell all right.'

'Put them in this bowl for me. Your pa told me that if the egg floats then it's bad, but it's easy enough to know for sure when you crack it open. Bad eggs smell awful.'

Whilst Davie and John entertained their sister she scrubbed both bedrooms and cleaned the windows. Joe was hammering and banging at the shelves and she prayed they would be usable when he'd finished.

Smoke had caught a further half a dozen mice upstairs and was prowling around with ears erect investigating every hole in the wall. There were definitely starlings living in the other chimney, but they were welcome to it. She was just thankful they hadn't taken residence in the kitchen stack.

She and Joe tacked pieces of wood taken from a packing case across the broken panes and already the cottage was a little warmer. It certainly smelt better. There was nothing she could do about the privy – an earth closet that hadn't been emptied when the last occupants had departed, and heaven knows how long ago that had been.

'Tomorrow, rain or shine, we've got to go to the farmhouse. I didn't see any workers in the fields today so I'm hoping they had the day off too.'

'You can't work in the fields, Ma, not with the baby.'

'I know that, John, so I'm expecting to work in the dairy or in the house – whatever Mrs Siddons requires. As there are cows I'm hoping we will get butter and milk tomorrow, which will make the hard work worthwhile.'

'Why don't you call her Grandma, Ma?' Davie asked.

'I don't know either of them. They've taken no interest in me or Alfie...' She hesitated, not sure if she should reveal the truth so soon after they'd lost their beloved father. 'We are here as free labour, in return for our board and lodging, not as members of the family. Don't expect to be treated any differently to any other day workers – in fact, you might well be worse off than them.'

The older boys exchanged glances but didn't seem surprised by her revelation. 'Don't worry about it, Ma, we'll not let you down. They ain't going to complain about us boys not doing our bit. We reckon they will be kinder to you and Mary because she's their blood, like,' Joe said.

Although they'd not managed to put any tiles back she and Joe had stopped the gaps with sacking, which wouldn't keep out the rain for long, but certainly made her bedroom less grim.

They retired early – she couldn't afford to keep the fire going into the evening or burn any of their precious oil or candles unnecessarily. They had reluctantly each used the privy before going up, but they had a chamber pot if they needed it during the night.

16

After the transaction took place at the bank, Alfie decided to bring the new owner of his business and home back to the cottage; this way Mr Daniel could be invited in as if visiting a friend and then he, Betty and the baby, could leave him in residence and stride away as if they were going for a day out.

The house was pristine. Betty was now wearing all three of her gowns and looked remarkably stout, but he doubted anyone would guess the reason for her roundness. There was also a basket filled with things Tommy would need until they had the opportunity to purchase more.

'It's a good thing you're still feeding him, Betty love. It means he won't go hungry wherever we are tonight.'

'What are you going to tell the boys when they come round?'

'Nothing at all. They won't care who they work for as long as they get paid for each delivery. If they don't know they can't blab about it.'

They had packed personal things away in the empty shed and he hoped one day it could be transported to wherever he and Betty were living. It fair broke his heart to leave behind the furniture what he'd made as he would never be able to make anything as good again. Mr Daniel was a good bloke and had agreed these items were on loan until they could be fetched. Betty was that upset to leave her china and linen, but these too were considered still to be their property.

'Right, I'm off to the bank to sign the papers. I'll bring the bloke back with me and then I'll get you to stitch the money into my coat and we'll be ready to leave.'

'What do I say if Mr Hatch comes round?'

'He ain't likely to. He'll be keeping his head down for a few days. But if he do, don't let him in. Tell him I've gone to meet a friend and will be back shortly and he's to come then to see me.'

Things was going too easy for his liking. To have found a buyer prepared to pay full price with no questions asked made him nervous. In his experience life weren't that good. Whatever his doubts, he wouldn't show them to Betty. It was his job to take care of this family, not add to their worries.

The torrential rain that had fallen yesterday had now eased off. The streets were slick and full of muddy puddles left over from the cattle market on Saturday. The cobbles were slippy at the best of times, but when wet they were bloody dangerous.

He signed the deeds with a flourish then had to wait whilst the chief cashier filled out each five-pound note by hand. Whilst they were waiting for this task to be completed he took Richard Daniel to one side. The man was half a head shorter than him but twice his weight, had a shock of brown hair and impressive whiskers. He were a clever gent and a tough one. Years as a sailor made him well able to take care of himself if need be.

'You're likely to get a visit from a cove called Hatch. He will want to know where I've gone, and might get nasty, but you ain't to tell him what he wants to know. I ain't going to tell you any forwarding address or even where we're going. Just tell Hatch as far as you know we've moved to London – which will be true – but you don't have no notion exactly whereabouts.'

'I thought it a rum do to get set up so quick, Mr Nightingale, but your hurry to leave is my good fortune. I never thought I'd find what I wanted so soon. I won't have to purchase anything extra. It will be hard for your missus to leave her fine furniture behind, but it's much appreciated, I can assure you.'

Finally, the fifteen notes were correctly filled in and they were able to depart. Alfie carefully divided the package into five and stowed each one in a different pocket in his voluminous coat. 'Righto, Mr Daniel, I need to get a move on as the train leaves in an hour.'

He strolled through the folk about their business, stopping to greet one or two known to him. He became aware that someone was following him as he turned into his own street. A prickle of fear ran down his spine. If he was attacked and robbed he would lose everything. He cursed under his breath that he hadn't got his dog by his side.

'There's trouble coming, Mr Daniel. Someone must have seen me put the money in my coat.'

'There's two of the bastards following us – I saw them watching through the window of the bank. Don't worry, I'll square up to anyone. I know how to take care of myself.'

Alfie surreptitiously released the buttons that held his coat together so he could slip his arms out of it when they were attacked. The two ruffians rushed them from behind, but he was ready.

The blow with a club aimed at the back of his head missed as he swayed sideways. He dropped his coat and kicked it aside not a second too soon. His attacker was shorter and leaner than him, his teeth black and his expression deadly. The second blow glanced across Alfie's shoulder but did no damage.

He landed a series of punches and the man staggered back. Daniel had a cut above his eye but was holding his own. Alfie began to believe they would come out of this relatively unhurt but then two more villains appeared and one of them was holding a loaded pistol.

Was this how he would die? To be murdered and robbed so close to safety was unbearable. How would Betty and little Tommy manage without him?

Then Buster hurtled past him and the fight was over. His dog savaged the man with the gun before he had the sense to pull the trigger – his companions didn't wait to receive the same treatment. The bastards who had started the attack hesitated a moment too long.

The dog tore into the one who had been attacking Alfie and the man's screams as he was bitten echoed down the empty road. Within moments doors were open and people were coming out to investigate.

'Buster, leave it. Good dog, leave.' Now the danger to his master had been dealt with the animal became a docile pet again. The blood dripping from his jaws and covering his chest made folk stand back in fear.

'That your animal, Mr Nightingale? Magnificent beast – I don't suppose he comes with the deal.'

'No, but there's a bloke down by the river has got a couple of dogs left what my dog fathered. I reckon he'll be glad we're moving on. It's the second litter his bitch has had thanks to Buster.'

'Then I'll get myself one. The animal's attracting a lot of attention so it might be best if we got him off the street and cleaned up.'

The men who'd been savaged had vanished, the only evidence remaining of their presence was the blood on the cobbles.

'Come along, Buster, let's get you home. How did you get out? I left you shut in the yard.' He picked up his discarded coat and shrugged it on again.

Daniel chuckled at his remarks. 'Not only does the dog save your life, he also appears to understand every word you say.'

'He's a clever one – knows what's what. I reckon he jumped over the wall at the back of the yard but I ain't no notion how he knew he was needed.'

Alfie knocked on the front door and Betty opened it immediately. Her hands flew to her mouth when she saw the state of both him, the new owner of the cottage, and the dog.

'It's all right, love, no real harm done – apart from to the bastards what tried to rob me.'

'Mr Daniel, you've got a nasty cut on your head. If you would care to sit down in the kitchen I'll tend to it for you.'

'Thank you, Mrs Nightingale, that would be much appreciated. If there's a cup of tea going, I could do with one after all that excitement.'

'I'll clean Buster, Betty, and then give meself a brush-down. We ain't got time for tea ourselves, but I'll brew it for you, Mr Daniel. You deserve a drink after what you went through on me behalf.'

Buster was happy to be washed down and dried with an old rag. By the time he'd done, the kettle was rattling on the range and he nipped into the kitchen to pour the boiling water onto the tea leaves. Betty had also finished and the damage to Mr Daniel's head wasn't as bad as it had looked now the blood had been cleaned off.

'We best be getting off, Betty love. You carry the basket and I'll take little Tommy. Buster don't need to be on the lead until we get to the station.'

He shook hands with the new owner of his little business and home. 'Take care, and don't get involved with Hatch like what I did.'

'I ain't a muttonhead, lad. I'll steer well clear of him. I aim to get a horse and cart – the fact that there's a stable and such at the back is the reason I was so keen to purchase your place.' He turned and patted Betty on the arm. 'Once you're settled, Nightingale, if you get in touch on the quiet like, I'll bring all your things to you on my cart.'

'Thank you, sir, your offer is much appreciated, but I'm not sure I'll ever be in a position to reclaim things.'

Little Tommy beamed at Alfie and patted his face when he picked him up. He looked around the cottage he'd thought would be his home for the next few years, the place he'd bought when he was almost sixteen years of age, and was now forced to leave because of that bastard. He vowed that one day the man what had driven him from his home would pay.

This time he didn't take the direct route to the river, across the bridge and into North Station Road, but walked to the High Street, and then turned right down North Hill. It would be a mile longer, but he doubted any of Hatch's minions would be looking out for him here. Word would have got out about the attack and it wouldn't take much for Hatch to work out that he was attacked because was carrying a deal of money about his person.

Enquiries would be made and within an hour or two the bastard would know everything and be on the hunt for them. With luck, they would be on the train and out of harm's way. The only problem with having Buster was that he was a memorable beast; anyone seeing him disembark from the train would remember.

He'd had the foresight to send a boy into the ramshackle building that sold tickets for the train so the ticket clerk wouldn't remember him. He'd bought three adult tickets – Buster didn't have to pay full price and Tommy went free. However, if an inspector wanted to see the tickets he couldn't cavil as Alfie had paid more than he should, not less.

Betty was unusually quiet and he glanced down at her. She was having difficulty holding back her tears. It was hard for her to leave the things she treasured behind. There was little expectation of them being able to send word to Daniel. As long as Hatch was alive they could have no contact with Colchester at all.

They arrived as the train was puffing in and he was able to hurry Betty and the dog into the designated carriage without being seen through the smoke and steam from the engine. They were the only occupants and for that he was grateful.

The guard waved his flag, the carriage lurched, and the train rattled out taking them to God knows where. He put his arm around his wife and she sobbed quietly on his shoulder.

'I'll make this up to you, Betty love. We'll rent somewhere better than the cottage in Maidenburgh Street and replace all the things you've lost.'

* * *

'Put the dirty dishes in the scullery, John. There's no time to attend to them this morning. I know it's barely light, but I'm sure I heard horses go by a few minutes ago.' Sarah was dreading the confrontation with her relatives, but was hoping if they all worked hard eventually her grandparents would accept the boys and they could move into the farmhouse and live as one family.

As she wasn't to be paid, that had been made clear in her initial conversation with her grandmother, how was she to buy the coal and other necessities that would be essential to keep her family alive and well during the long winter months? Unless they were able to reside with her grandparents they would not survive

– there wouldn't be sufficient timber in the surrounding copses and fields to maintain the fire. The small amount of money she had should be kept for emergencies only.

The fire was banked down and hopefully would remain smouldering until they returned for their midday meal. They should be fed in the farmhouse, but she doubted they would be invited in.

The ground was crisp underfoot; there had been a heavy frost last night. The boys were as well wrapped up as they could be. They had warm jackets, stout boots, mufflers and fingerless mittens. She was more concerned about Mary. The baby was snug enough at the moment beneath her cloak, but would want to get down at some point and if they were outside in the fields this would be impossible.

'Cor, look at that, Ma. Two big horses are in the yard. What are they for?' Davie asked.

'I expect that they have come to pull the plough. I believe such things take place at this time of year.'

There was no sign of the men who had brought the horses to the farm. They must be in one of the sheds or barns. 'Wait here, boys. Stay out of the wind, whilst I go and find out what we have to do this morning.'

'Them cows need milking, Ma. I can hear them in the barn. I wouldn't mind being learnt to do that,' Joe said with a grin. He was the only one apparently eager to begin his servitude.

The farmhouse was in good repair, the windows clean, the paintwork freshly done and the roof with no holes in it. In fact, now she saw the buildings clearly, she could see the place looked quite prosperous.

She walked briskly across the hard-packed dirt that made up the yard in front of the building, grateful it had frozen solid and was no longer wet and muddy. Her knock was answered immediately by a surly individual in a grubby smock.

'The missus says them boys are to let the pigs out and clean the sty. You're to go to the dairy and churn the butter.' He closed the door in her face before she could ask any questions.

'Now we know what we are to do, we can get started. I shall collect you when it's time for a break. You will get dirty and smelly but must not complain.'

John hung back and for a horrible moment she thought he would refuse to go with his brothers; then he straightened his shoulders, smiled bravely, and trotted off behind them. Dan would be horrified to think his beloved boys were reduced to this – little better than slaves.

Presumably the dairy was somewhere close to where the cows were lowing so she made her way in that direction. She could hear the clatter of pails and headed for that building. When she pushed open the door she saw a young girl, probably not much older than Joe, busy stirring something in a wooden vat.

'Good morning. I'm here to help you. I'm Mrs Cooper, granddaughter to Mr and Mrs Siddons.'

The girl nodded. 'I'm Jenny. I'm cutting the curd; you fetch the hot whey from the copper and bring it here.'

Sarah wasn't quite sure what whey was but did know a copper when she saw one. There was an enamelled jug standing beside this and she assumed that was what she had to use. She pulled back the lid and dipped it into the hot, creamy liquid.

'Tip that in here. We need to get the curd cooked.'

After an hour Mary protested about being restrained and Sarah thought the dairy warm enough to let her toddle about in her bare feet. 'I need to put my baby down for a bit. Will that be all right?'

For the first time the girl smiled. 'I never knew you had a babe under that cloak, missus. You put her down – she'll come to no harm in here.'

The next few hours were spent repeating the process until the dairymaid announced that the curd was ready. Although this process had been strenuous, in between bouts of activity Sarah had ample opportunity to take care of her daughter. She prayed the boys were getting on as well as she was.

'It's got to be piled up one end and covered in a cloth. Then we drain off the whey and it goes to the pigs.'

'Jenny, what time do we stop to eat? Mary will need feeding soon and she certainly needs changing.'

'This has to be turned and stacked three times. I can do that – I'll need you to help when we put it in the press. Mrs Siddons told me you would be working in here in future instead of Molly, but she never told me nothing about when you should take your break.'

'I'll go now, and be back within the hour. I shall collect the boys and make sure they are fed as well.'

'I shouldn't do that. Them boys will be expected to work through until they've finished.'

Sarah wasn't going to argue with this girl, but neither was she going to leave her children without food and a hot drink.

The foul stench from the pigs made it easy for her to find the three of them. They were filthy, John was blue with cold and Davie little better. Only Joe appeared to be dealing with the situation.

'Put your shovels somewhere tidy, boys, and return to the cottage as soon as you can. You will have to eat your lunch in the outhouse, but at least you will be out of the wind and getting something hot inside you.'

She didn't wait for a response but hurried off. She wanted to fill the copper and set a fire under it so there would be enough hot water for them to have a bath when they had finished for the day. This would be a wicked extravagance and use up the meagre supply of coal she had brought with her – but tonight they would be clean, although she feared it might well be the last time any of them was able to take a bath.

Spot emerged from the trees and trotted beside her. Mary clapped her hands and tried to reach down to pat the dog. 'Just a minute, sweetheart, you can play with him when we are inside.'

The kitchen was warm and it took only a few minutes to push the kettle and stewpot over the flames to heat up. There was no time to remove her boots even though they would make the flags filthy – but needs must.

When the boys clattered into the yard their food was ready and she was just tipping a third lot of water into the copper. Even Joe was silent. She blinked back tears at the state of them. They weren't used to doing such heavy manual work and it wasn't right that John, only six years of age, should be doing such things.

'I put water in the outhouse and some rags. Get yourselves as clean as you can and I'll bring out your food.'

They trooped miserably into the outhouse and she returned to the task of dishing up the stew into tin bowls and pouring out three mugs of tea. She put a chunk of bread by each dish and then picked up the tray. 'Spot, take care of Mary. Make sure she doesn't go near the fire.' Asking the dog to protect her baby was ridiculous, but he was an intelligent animal like his father and would keep her daughter safe from harm for the few minutes it would take her to deliver the food.

The boys were slumped on the floor – thank God she'd had the foresight to put sacks down or they would be sitting on the dirt.

'Here you are, boys. I'll put the tray on the ground and you must help yourself. As soon as you've eaten and used the privy if necessary, you must go back and complete your task. The work will get easier as you get stronger – remember what Uncle Alfie told you about the time he spent shovelling coal on the River Thames. It took him a week or two, but then the work became easier.'

None of them replied and she daren't remain outside any longer in case Mary went near the fire. As she ran back to the cottage she wished she had ignored the stink and given them all a hug. It wasn't their fault they were covered in pig muck and they needed all the comfort they could get.

She gobbled down her own stew whilst feeding Mary from the same bowl with the other hand. 'Sit in your chair, love, and finish your bread. I'm just going to the privy.'

There was no sound from the building the boys were in but her need was urgent so she couldn't look in until after she'd done what was necessary. The smell from the earth closet was mild in comparison to that of the children.

After adjusting her skirts she went to speak to them but they had gone. The bowls and mugs were empty and neatly stacked on the tray. At least they wouldn't go without sustenance all day as Mrs Siddons had intended.

* * *

She was back at the dairy in less than the allotted hour but the place was deserted. The girl had obviously completed the task and gone elsewhere. The place was pristine, the floor freshly scrubbed, and Sarah didn't know what she should do next. She had no option but to go to the farmhouse and enquire.

This time she went to the back door and didn't knock. She pushed it open and stepped into a flagged passageway. To the right was a scullery and pantry; to the left a door that must lead to the kitchen itself.

From the clatter and sound of voices there were several people inside. She pushed open the door and what hope she had of being accepted at Hockley Farm shrivelled inside her. Sitting around the central table were her grandparents plus what were obviously their five labourers. She and the boys should have been here too and not obliged to find their own meal.

She had made a dreadful mistake coming to Hockley Farm. She should have stayed with Alfie and Betty, but it was too late to repine. She didn't have the wherewithal to return and must make the best she could of this disaster.

'Mrs Siddons, I wish to know what I should do next.' She was proud her voice was even, that her misery wasn't apparent.

'Tell those brats of yours when they've done with the pigs they can go down to the field and pick stones. There's laundry to be done so you'd best get on with it.'

None of the workers were looking in her direction and for that she was grateful. Sarah nodded but didn't reply and marched out, leaving them to their hot meal and comfortable surroundings.

She delivered the message to her sons who nodded miserably and then she went in search of the wash house. At least she wasn't obliged to do this work outside as the farmhouse had a built-on laundry room. It was warm in here and Mary could be put down. It was several years since she'd been obliged to do any heavy work like this, but she was young and fit and was having a far easier time of it than the boys.

Her grandparents were obviously well off as they wouldn't have this place if they weren't. She came to an unpleasant but necessary decision. She wasn't going to be paid for her work, and it didn't seem as if the food they were all entitled to was to be offered. Therefore, if she was going to keep her family alive over the winter she would have to take what she needed.

This wouldn't be stealing – not really. They should all have their food provided and be decently housed as were the other farmworkers. Taking food, fuel and anything else that was needed would be her wages.

By the time she had finished pounding clothes in the tub with a dolly stick and putting them through the mangle, she was exhausted and Mary had fallen asleep. She hung the sheets and other items on the poles that stretched across the ceiling and was done.

'Come along, little one, time to go home.' When she picked up her baby she was horrified to find Mary's clothes were sodden where she'd been lying in a puddle. She put the baby beneath her cloak and hurried to the cottage. The air was cold. There would be another hard frost tonight.

17

———————

'We'll be pulling into Chelmsford soon, Betty love. We need to disembark quickly and get off the station before anyone notices us. I think you should go first and then Buster and I will follow a few minutes later.'

'That's all very well, Alfie, but where am I to go? I reckon you should go and then I'll follow. Here, give me our Tommy. Folk would notice if they see a man carrying his child.'

'You can't manage the baby and the basket...'

'Well, I'll just have to, won't I? You go on with the dog and then wait for me.'

'I'll do that. Hatch might well send men to make enquiries along the line, but they will be asking after three of us, and hopefully splitting up will do the trick.'

The train lurched to a halt and this time his dog were not restrained. The animal were well trained and if he told him to go on ahead he would do so. This would hopefully confuse the searchers even more.

He'd already given Betty her ticket and he had his own in his hand. As soon as the door was open he told his dog to run off and

Buster vanished. He handed in his ticket and left the station. No one would have known he owned a dog or had a wife – he was just a gent out for a stroll.

He walked rapidly until he was a goodly distance from where the trains halted and then paused as if admiring the square. There were a domed thing with columns and a fancy roof in the centre of this space, but it didn't seem to have any purpose that he could see.

Buster was cocking his leg against it and he didn't blame him. He waited until Betty caught up with him. 'Says that this is Tindal Square and that over there is the Saracens Head Hotel. It's a coaching inn and should have overnight accommodation. We'll go there and book ourselves a room.'

'What about your dog? You can hardly take him in with you.'

'I'll give a stable lad a tanner and he'll take care of him. Tomorrow we'll find ourselves somewhere decent to rent.'

A coach had just pulled under the archway and the yard was busy with passengers getting in and out of the vehicle. It was easy to mingle with them and find a boy to take care of Buster.

'You stay out here; I'll be back tomorrow,' Alfie told his dog and the animal thumped his tail as if understanding the words.

There were so many people in the vestibule he was forced to draw Betty to one side until the harassed landlord had time to deal with them. Once the space was clear and the stagecoach had departed, Alfie stepped forward. 'I need a room with a parlour for a few nights. I'm looking to rent somewhere decent in the town and will need to stop here until I find what I'm looking for.'

The man wiped his hands on his apron. 'I have a fine room at the back – you and your wife won't be disturbed there. Will you be requiring meals?'

'That we will. We are sharp-set as we've been travelling since yesterday – we've come down from London today to make a new start.' Only then did Alfie think about their lack of luggage and how this would draw unwanted attention to them. 'Our belongings are in transit. They will be arriving tomorrow or the next day and I need to have the house to put them in by then.'

The man dipped his pen in the inkwell and held it poised above the empty space in the ledger. 'What names should I put, sir?'

'Mr and Mrs Jack Rand from St Albans.'

The man scratched this onto the page and then swivelled the book so Alfie could sign his fictitious signature. He dipped into his pocket and produced a single gold coin. 'This will pay my account for the next day or two.'

The landlord beamed and the coin vanished into his pocket. He then rang the small brass bell standing on the countertop and a bootboy came at a run. 'Jimmy, take Mrs Rand to the chambers overlooking the garden. Have hot water fetched and get the kitchen to send up a selection of whatever is available at the moment.'

The boy touched his forelock. 'Follow me, ma'am, it's a right fine set of rooms you're having.'

'Go along, Betty love. I'll be up in a few minutes.'

The landlord closed the book now the ink was dry and rubbed his substantial belly. 'How big a property are you looking for, Mr Rand?'

'Four bedrooms at least, a decent kitchen, scullery and boot room, two reception rooms and a garden for my little lad to play in when he's bigger.'

'Then I think that I can help you. I'll send word to the landlord of the property I'm thinking of and, if it's still vacant, then you and Mrs Rand can inspect it first thing tomorrow morning.'

Alfie shook hands and then dashed after his wife. The suite of chambers was as good as he'd hoped – far grander than anything he'd ever stayed in.

Betty was wandering around exclaiming in delight. 'Look at this. I'll feel like a princess sleeping here tonight. The boy said they'll lay up the table over there under the window and we can eat on that. The bedroom has a fire lit in it already and the bed is clean and the linen aired.' Then her smile slipped and she frowned. 'Can we afford this, Alfie? You have no business to bring us in money at the moment.'

'We can't stop here for more than a night or two, but I've paid up front for that. We deserve a treat. Let's enjoy it and not count the cost just for now.'

* * *

There was no sign of the boys when she arrived at the cottage. They should have been back by now as it was almost dark and they could hardly be picking stones in the fields when they couldn't see their hands in front of their faces.

First she must strip off the baby and get her warm and then she would worry about the others.

'Mary, sweetheart, wake up for your ma. I'm going to give you a nice hot bath in front of the fire and then you can have your tea.'

The baby didn't stir and she was worryingly cold to the touch. When she was snugly wrapped Sarah put her down in front of the fire, the only place in this horrible cottage that was warm. She fetched the small tin bath and put it on the table and then scooped out two buckets of hot water from the copper and tipped them in.

The sound of purring was coming from the floor and Smoke was nudging Mary and patting her with a paw. Her daughter's eyes opened and she gurgled and reached out to stroke the animal. The icy dread that had gripped her since she picked Mary from the puddle began to dissipate.

'Well then, little one, are you ready for your bath?'

It was hard to remain low-spirited when bathing a baby. The cat retreated not enjoying being splashed, but seeing this precious child restored to her usual self made Sarah forget about her circumstances for a moment or two.

There was a noise outside the back door and Joe yelled through the window. 'We're going to strip off out here, Ma. You don't want the stinking clothes inside.'

'Wait a minute, I'll bring you some sacks you can put on to preserve your modesty.' She lifted a wet wriggling baby from the water and wrapped her in the towel that had been warming in front of the fire. 'Your brothers are back, sweetheart. I must get their bath ready now.'

* * *

The three of them used the water in Mary's bath to wash the worst of the pig muck from their persons and then Joe took it outside and tipped it somewhere – hopefully not anywhere it would freeze and cause them to slip and break their necks tomorrow.

'John's going first, then Davie, then me. We'll empty it for you when we're done, Ma.'

'Good boy. Could you do something else for me please? I need you to feed Mary whilst I slip out for a bit.'

He didn't question where she was going, but handed her the basket with a wink. 'We'll be just fine. We was late getting home tonight because we collected some firewood. We put it in the lean-to so it can dry out.'

If he hadn't smelt so bad she would have given him a hug. She put on her cloak, mittens and muffler and made her way stealthily back to the dairy. She had already put a jug in her basket and intended to help herself to milk and anything else that she could find.

Although it was dark there was a bright moon, which gave her sufficient light to see where she was going. She collected a dozen eggs from the barn, helped herself to potatoes, carrots and turnips from the vegetable store, but couldn't find anything else in the darkness.

She was ashamed of herself for resorting to stealing food from her grandparents, but she would do anything to keep her family fed even if it meant she risked transportation or worse if she was discovered. The fact that she was related to the farmers would make no difference – she was certain Mrs Siddons would take pleasure in handing her over to the parish constable.

It wasn't until she was almost home, Spot trotting beside her, that something occurred to her. She wasn't in the wrong; they were. Anyone who laboured on a farm was entitled to be fed and housed or paid a few shillings a week in lieu of accommodation. All she was getting was this dismal cottage – no food, no fuel, and no remuneration.

This made her feel happier about what she had just done. Tomorrow, somehow, she would get into the farmhouse and find some candles, flour and lard to make pastry and bread. She had brought sufficient with her to keep them going for a week, but after that they would go hungry if she didn't take what was owed to her.

The boys were reluctant to show her the damage their day's work had inflicted but she insisted on examining their blistered hands and applying salve to them. 'Tomorrow, you must wrap them in strips of cloth to keep them clean. Did Mr Siddons tell you that you are to take care of the pigs?'

John had fallen asleep with his head on the table; Davie was little better, so Joe answered for them. 'No, we never saw either of them. The cowman was the only person spoke to us all day. Even the ploughmen ignored us, but it won't be so bad, once we've got used to it, Ma. The worst part is the smell, I reckon.' He yawned and his jaw cracked. 'We like the pigs. They're clever beasts and John spent a lot of the time scratching them on the back with his shovel.'

'Can you wake up your brother and help him to bed? I'll bank up the fire, and then I'll be up too.'

Tonight she was so bone-weary she fell asleep immediately despite the cold and damp. As she was drifting off she wondered what Alfie and Betty were doing and prayed she would have an opportunity to send a message to them.

Remaining here was not an option; they must return to Colchester at the earliest possible opportunity. Being cramped in Alfie's little cottage would be like paradise after this.

* * *

After spending the night in luxury Betty was expecting Alfie to find her a home of a similar standard. However, Alfie weren't comfortable with all the fuss and trimmings and was determined to find something less grand. It would have to be bigger than the cottage in Colchester, but not one of them new houses being built what the landlord had told him about.

He left his wife with the baby viewing the emporiums and set out to explore what was going to become his new home. Chelmsford weren't as big as Colchester, he didn't think, but it were prosperous enough. They held a market every week, which meant if he got hold of a barrow or two, and a couple of lads to push them, he could make a bit – but not enough to support them comfortably.

He was walking down the High Street and stopped to look in the window of what looked like a shop that sold ready-made ladies' garments. He'd never bought anything new in his life; there was always something to be found on a second-hand stall. Shirts and undergarments were sewn by the womenfolk of the family, as well as the one or two gowns they owned.

He'd never seen a place where women could buy things – there was a factory in Colchester what made men's garments; both his ma and step-pa had worked for Mr Hyam and his brothers. He peered through the glass and saw the place was open, but empty. He would step inside and see if he could purchase something for Betty as she'd had to leave so much behind.

He pushed open the door and the little bell rang. Immediately there was the sound of someone hurrying from the workshop at the back. He gripped the countertop and his knees all but gave way beneath him.

'Ma? Is that you? It's Alfie. I can't believe I walked into the very place you're working in.'

The woman he'd recognised immediately looked stunned, but recovered quickly and ran forward to throw her arms around him. 'Alfie? My, how you've grown. You're a handsome man and no mistake. I never thought to see either you or Sarah again.'

'I thought you and Rand moved to London. What are you doing in Chelmsford?'

'Jack is dead; he died two years ago. I didn't want to stay in London, but when I visited Colchester and spoke to Martha Sainty – you remember she lived next door to us in East Stockwell Street – she said you had never come back after Tommy died and that Sarah was no longer at Grey Friars.'

'I did come back, Ma, but it were after your visit and Sarah was in Colchester until a few weeks ago. She was married to a good man who died in an accident in September.' He told her everything that had transpired over the past few years and she told him that she owned the business – wasn't an employee.

'Jack was killed by an omnibus and he was paid compensation. I bought this place with the money. It's bigger than it looks and has a pretty garden at the back where the children can play.'

His mother locked the door so that no customers could come in in her absence and took him on a quick tour of the property. Downstairs there was the shop, a decent-sized workroom in which there were two young seamstresses busy sewing, and behind that there were a kitchen that ran the width of the house and was well appointed. The house was double-fronted, and there was a sitting room, a second smaller parlour and four generous-sized bedrooms. More than enough for all of them.

Outside was a large yard, a privy, and a couple of outbuildings that would be ideal for workshops and to house the dogs. There was a patch of grass with borders around it – although they were empty at the moment. He couldn't believe his luck.

Once he'd been shown everywhere he hugged his mother. 'I'll go and find my Betty, and bring her round. I'll write to Sarah, send her the money for the fare, and she should be with us in a week or two.'

'There's sufficient furniture upstairs for you and Betty, but there's no cradle, so your little one will have to sleep in one of the drawers from the chest.'

'He'll do just fine in that, Ma. I won't be long – I just have to find Betty and settle up at the Saracens.'

'I'll send one of my girls out for provisions. There'll be luncheon waiting for you when you get here.'

The bell tinkled as he exited and Alfie felt like breaking into song. Fancy Ma being a widow, and a wealthy one at that. What with his money and hers they could make a good life together. All they needed was to have Sarah and her children safe back in the family again.

He'd left Buster in the stables and not mentioned to Ma that there would be two enormous hounds as part of this household too.

He discovered his wife had returned to the hotel and was drinking tea in the snug. When he explained, she was speechless.

'The good Lord above has answered my prayers, Alfie love. It's nothing short of a blooming miracle – that's what it is.' She was on her feet and, with the baby dangling on her hip, she raced away to collect their few belongings.

The landlord grudgingly returned a few shillings and with Buster at his side they were ready to begin their new life.

'When will it be safe to send for our things? I'd like to have my own linen and such if that's possible.'

'Not for a while, Betty love – better let the dust settle. Mr Daniel said he would pack everything away outside in the workshop and bring it over in the spring in his new cart.'

'At least I shall have a spare gown or two. I can sew, but not well enough to be a seamstress. When Sarah arrives, she can work with your ma and I'll take care of the children and the household.'

'I reckon we'll be able to afford for someone to come in and do the heavy work. We've gone up in the world; make no mistake about that.'

* * *

That night they ate together in the parlour in front of a roaring fire. Betty and his ma hit it off immediately and were now as thick as thieves. The baby settled happily in his temporary cradle and whilst the womenfolk chatted he set about writing the letter to his sister.

Sarah,

I'm sending you the money to pay for your removal from Hockley Farm. We are going to live with our ma in Chelmsford where she has bought a substantial business. Jack Rand died and left her comfortable.

I look forward to seeing you and the boys and baby Mary here at the above address as soon as may be.

Your loving brother,

Alfie

He had always had a neat hand and although he wrote slowly and laboriously he was able to produce a respectable letter with few mistakes. He smiled as he blotted it dry. It were a pity he didn't speak as proper as he wrote.

He folded the paper around the money and pushed it into the envelope. He would take it to the post office himself tomorrow morning and have it sent by express. That way he could be sure Sarah would receive it and the money wouldn't be removed before it arrived at the farm.

18

Several days passed, each more depressing than the last. Sarah had had no opportunity to get into the farmhouse to replenish her dwindling stocks of flour, lard and meat. She had not spoken to either of her relatives. Instructions were relayed to her via the taciturn dairymaid – Jenny.

The weather was miserable. Icy east winds blew in from the sea and the three boys were suffering dreadfully. They all had blistered hands and even the rags and mittens they wore were not sufficient protection.

By Friday they had no bread and were relying on the dog to bring them a rabbit. The boys were also pilfering whatever they could and there was a marked improvement in the health of the chickens and the chicks since they had been getting regular feeds of grain stolen from the yard.

Their breakfast of hot milk and baked potato was filling and not a scrap was left. Even Joe had lost his enthusiasm for farming and there was no chatter as they ate.

She couldn't bear to see her boys so miserable. 'If the weather improves I think we should walk back to Colchester. I should never have brought you here...'

'It's not your fault, Ma, that we've been forced to live here and don't get paid for our work,' Joe said.

'You don't understand, Joe, I knew that my grandparents only wanted us to come as free labour. But I thought once they saw us they would soften in their attitude and make us welcome.' She looked from one to the other, but their expressions were apathetic. They seemed uninterested in anything she said.

'We don't have to work on Sunday – I thought if the weather remains dry we will leave. It is no more than ten miles and we should be able to achieve that distance before it gets dark.'

John was so exhausted he had fallen asleep again at the table. Would he be able to walk that far in his present debilitated condition?

'I'm going to speak to Mrs Siddons this morning and demand that we are given the rations we are owed. I am not going to steal anything else and neither should you. They are the ones who are breaking the law by not giving us what we are due.'

She looked at her youngest son and came to a decision. 'John, you stay here today.' The little boy sat up and, for the first time since they arrived, he smiled. 'No, all of you will remain here. Do you think that you could take care of Mary between you whilst I am working?'

Joe nodded eagerly. 'We can do that for you, Ma. She's good as gold with us. If we don't have to work again, we'll be right enough to get back to Colchester on Sunday.'

'There's still some stew in the pot for lunch but we are out of coal and I'm not sure that the wood will be hot enough to boil a kettle.'

Sarah was accustomed to her duties in the dairy now. They only had half a dozen cows so there wasn't sufficient milk to warrant Mr Siddons having a diligence and horse deliver it around the villages. Therefore, once the farm and the workers had taken what they needed each day, the remainder was either made into cheese or churned for butter.

Her tasks in the dairy would be completed by lunchtime and she was then expected to do whatever laundry had been accumulated. Today, as she hadn't got the baby to carry, she brought up a sack full of the boys' clothes and intended to get them clean before she did anything for her grandmother.

They hadn't been working long when the cowman came in. 'Where's them boys of yours? Them pigs need feeding and cleaning.'

'They won't be coming again until Monday. They are not indentured servants; they are my sons, and I'm not having them exploited in this way.'

The man didn't argue, merely shrugged and stomped off. Jenny, however, had plenty to say on the matter.

'The missus won't like that. We don't get no days off here apart from Sunday.'

'It's none of your concern, Jenny. I thank you to get on with your own business.' Sarah carefully removed her apron. 'I'm going out. I'll be back in an hour.'

She swirled her cloak around her shoulders and set out to confront her grandmother. She was determined that she wouldn't return to the dairy, or to the cottage, until she'd had her demands met.

As she reached the back door Spot appeared at her side. She was about to send the dog away, but reconsidered. He would be ideal if Mrs Siddons proved difficult. She knocked, but didn't wait to be invited in.

She marched through the boot room and pushed open the kitchen door. As she paused the dog pressed against her side. She could feel his tension through the thickness of her clothes. Her quarry was standing at the kitchen range stirring a pot of soup.

'I have come to collect what I'm owed, Mrs Siddons. You have had labour from four of us for four days and we have had nothing in return. I'm going to fill up my basket with what I need from your pantry.'

The woman opened her mouth but no words came out. Spot was growling deep in his throat and that was enough to keep her quiet. Sarah first took bacon, ham, flour and lard and then picked up a freshly baked loaf of bread and a slab of cheese. They already had butter and milk taken yesterday.

Throughout this process her grandmother remained in front of the range. Although she said nothing, her expression was murderous.

'Thank you, Mrs Siddons. I shall send the boys to collect coal and logs for the fires. I shall be doing my own laundry this after-noon as my boys have nothing clean to wear.'

There was so much in the basket she could scarcely lift it from the kitchen table. 'By law you should be feeding and housing us and also giving us monetary recompense. The cottage we are obliged to reside in is little better than a hovel and so far we have received nothing from you. What I am taking is a fraction of what we are owed.'

Still her adversary remained silent. Sarah retraced her steps and hurried back to the cottage with her bounty. 'Good dog, in future I shall keep you with me as without your protection I doubt I would get what I need.'

Everything was peaceful inside. Mary had fallen asleep on a blanket in front of the fire with John, and Davie and Joe were busy in the scullery with the breakfast dishes. They were suitably impressed with her largesse.

'Me and Davie will go and get a sack of coal now,' Joe said as he wiped his mouth on his sleeve after having consumed three slices of bread and jam.

'Take the dog with you. I'll stay here until you return, but then I must go to the laundry and get your clothes clean.'

* * *

In less than half an hour she was walking briskly along the rutted lane. The sun was out, although it had little warmth in it. She couldn't help smiling. As long as the weather held she would leave this dreadful place with her family on Sunday morning. She would have to abandon the furniture and other items she had brought with her, but it would be worth it to be away from here.

There was somebody in the laundry room – no doubt Mrs Siddons had sent the kitchen maid to do the work that Sarah had refused to do. She pushed open the door and was met by a fusillade of blows. She reeled back, lost her footing and crashed to the cobbles.

Her grandmother stood over her, fists clenched. 'You bitch, do you think you can come here and steal from me? You're no better than your mother and we were well rid of her. I want you gone from here or I'll have the constables on you.'

The woman raised her booted foot and Sarah braced herself, knowing she was about to be viciously kicked. Then everything changed. Her grandfather appeared and grabbed hold of his wife.

'No, Elsie, I'll not have it. You get inside or it will be you who gets kicked.' He shoved his wife towards the back door and she staggered, almost falling, but didn't argue.

Sarah pushed herself onto her elbows too shaken and bruised to attempt to stand.

'Let me help you. This is my fault – Elsie's not right in the head. I should've stood up to her, insisted you and the children moved in with us where you belong.'

He offered his hand but she ignored it. When she put her hand on the back of her head it came away red and sticky – but she wasn't dizzy any more and was sure she wasn't badly hurt.

'I can manage, thank you.' When she was upright, she shook out her skirts. 'We have been here for almost a week and you have done nothing to help us. It's too late now to step in when the damage has been done.'

She turned to enter the laundry room but he prevented her. 'No point in going in there, Sarah – Elsie's destroyed your clothes. There is nothing left for you to launder.'

She clutched the door frame. The woman was certainly deranged and the sooner they were away from here the better. Somehow, she managed the walk home but by the time she went into the kitchen her eyes were blurred and her legs would no longer support her.

* * *

Several days elapsed and there had been no word from Sarah, and Alfie was becoming concerned. 'Something ain't right, Ma. She should've been here by now. I daren't go back meself as Hatch will be looking out for me.'

'Is there someone in Colchester you could contact who would be prepared to go out to Great Bromley and see what's keeping them?'

'I'll write to Robert Billings – he's a good sort of cove. If he's not at sea he'll be happy to do that for me.'

He scribbled a note and took it directly to the post office and sent it by express. It were to be delivered into the hands of his friend. If he weren't there the letter would be returned and then he'd have to contact the man who'd bought his cottage and ask him to do him this favour.

The following morning, he was just returning from his morning constitutional with Buster when the postman arrived at the shop door. 'Is that for me?'

'If you're Mr Alfie Nightingale, then it is. Sign here please.'

He didn't recognise the scrawl on the envelope, but it certainly weren't his own letter come back to him.

Alfie,

I'm going to fetch Sarah and the boys and bring them to you in Chelmsford. We should be with you late this evening or first thing tomorrow morning.

Robert

He burst through the door, making the bell almost fly from its spring. Ma and Betty rushed in. He waved the paper at them. 'Robert's going to fetch them.'

'Thank the good Lord for that,' Ma said. 'She should never have gone out there. My pa was a reasonable man but my ma had a vicious temper. I got away from them as soon as I could. I should have told you both the truth and then she would never have gone.'

'She'll be all right, don't fret. She's got Spot, Buster's son – he'll protect her. I reckon she never got my letter and doesn't know we're waiting for her. One of them must have got to it first.'

'That must be the reason, Alfie love. We've been worrying needlessly.'

It had been his task to purchase the beds and such that they needed to furnish the rooms they would be occupying. There'd been a furniture sale at a big house and he'd picked up some decent bits and pieces. Betty were pleased with what he'd bought.

There hadn't been much more for him to do, apart from exercising his dog and searching the second-hand stalls and pawn-shops for the tools he needed to work again. He'd found a decent timber merchant down by the railway and had put in an order, which was being delivered at any moment.

There was a gate at the bottom of the garden, which opened onto the lane just wide enough for a cart to get down, if it weren't too big. They couldn't keep a pig in the middle of town but he intended to buy half a dozen pullets at the next market. He'd already adapted one of the outbuildings for them to live in.

'I'm off down the yard. Me wood's arriving soon and I want to get it stowed away. Then I'll get started on some of them high chairs what did so well in Colchester.'

'You go on then, Alfie love. Your ma and I have plenty to do. It's a real shame those handsome beds you made for the boys won't be coming with them.'

'They'll manage with the ones I got from the sale. They're going to need new garments and suchlike. Are you going to make them, Ma?'

'That I am, son. I'd not thought of sewing children's clothes, but I think there might be a market for ready-made jackets and trousers. Most women can make petticoats, shirts and dresses for the girls so I'll not bother with them.' She smiled and gestured around her immaculate workroom where the two girls was already busy at their work. 'You don't need to worry about money. I'm well set up and making more than enough to keep us all in comfort. But you go on and make your bits and pieces if that's what you want to do.'

Betty nodded happily. 'When Sarah comes, she will be designing and cutting like your ma, and the business will prob-ably need two more girls in the workshop. I'm going to run the house and take care of the children – I can't tell you how happy I am to be settled so soon.'

Alfie managed a smile but he weren't happy about what she'd said. He was the man of the house. It was his job to provide for the family not the womenfolk. He flexed his damaged hand. It looked all right but he couldn't grip proper for long without pain. He would never be a craftsman again – and just making a few simple items wouldn't bring in enough income to make much difference.

The boys would go back to school – that had already been talked about. He would have no role to play in this new household apart from being Betty's husband and Tommy's father. He weren't the kind of gent to be satisfied with that. He wanted to be respected by his family, to do something useful, but he couldn't think what that might be.

One thing was for certain: he weren't going back to being a criminal. From now on he would find himself an honest occupation so his boy could grow up proud of him.

* * *

Sarah wanted to reassure the boys but her head was too muddled. One of them pulled out a chair and she collapsed onto it. Their voices seemed far away and she couldn't quite grasp what they were telling her. Then it was as if she fell into a dark hole and she remembered nothing more until she woke up stretched out on the kitchen floor.

'Ma, Ma, Joe's gone to find help. Stop where you are.' Davie's face loomed over her and she tried to summon a smile.

'Mary?'

'She's fast asleep upstairs. She don't know nothing about this. Joe and I have put a bandage round your injury and it doesn't seem to be bleeding too much no more.'

She was warm and comfortable where she was and had no

wish to move. Perhaps if she had a nice rest, when she awoke she would be able to get up.

From a distance there were voices she didn't recognise – male voices. Then she was picked up and enveloped in a blanket. The world went black again.

When she next opened her eyes she was in a comfortable bed. Clean linen surrounded her and the chamber was warm.

'Thank God you are awake at last, Sarah. The doctor said you might never wake up after such a head injury.'

She blinked a few times and slowly brought her gaze to rest on the speaker. 'Mr Siddons? Am I in the farmhouse? I don't understand...'

Her grandfather moved closer and patted her hands. There were tears trickling down his wrinkled cheeks. 'Your grandma isn't here any more. I've had her put in an asylum – I should have done it years ago. She'll not hurt anyone else.' He wiped his eyes on a somewhat wrinkled handkerchief. 'Your boys and your baby are being taken care of by the woman I've brought in from the village to run the house.'

This was too much to take in. She closed her eyes whilst she thought about what he'd told her. She and her family were finally safe and had the home she'd hoped for. That the woman who had almost killed her was a lunatic – not responsible for her actions – this was harder to believe.

She attempted to turn her head and regretted it. 'She seemed perfectly sane to me, just thoroughly unpleasant and cold-hearted. It wasn't until she attacked me that she showed any signs of mania.'

'Don't you fret about it now, Sarah, just get well. You've got sutures in your head that have to be removed and the doctor is coming to see you later.'

There was a sound behind him and three small faces

appeared. 'Boys, I'm pleased to see you. I'll be up and about again soon so make sure you take care of your sister, behave yourselves and do what you're told.'

Joe ushered his brothers forward until they were within reach. 'It's grand here, Ma. Grandpa says we don't have to work, that we're family. He's had our beds and things moved here and Mary's got her own bed now; she don't have to share with John.'

Sarah attempted to stretch out and touched his hand but for some reason hadn't the energy. 'That's wonderful, sweetheart. As soon as I'm better you can show me around.'

Davie shuffled closer. 'Spot's allowed in the kitchen but nowhere else. We've brung them hens and chicks here and they're doing fine with the others in the barn.'

John didn't speak but squeezed her hand. 'Thank you for visiting, boys, but I need to rest. Come and see me later.'

Once they had gone she looked for her grandfather but he was no longer there. Instead there was a girl, not much older than the dairymaid, hovering in the background. She curtsied which, if her head hadn't hurt so abominably, Sarah would have found ridiculous.

'I've got barley water, hot milk or tea – the doctor said you were to drink as much as possible.'

'Barley water, but first I have to use the commode.'

Getting upright was nigh impossible but her need was desperate and somehow between them she managed to roll from the bed onto the chair with the pot in it just in time to avoid an embarrassing accident.

If she had a concussion, why wasn't she sick? Her head hurt, but not unbearably, so she didn't think she had been seriously injured. So why was she so feeble?

After she was safely back in her bed she asked the young

attendant. 'Do you know what the doctor said had happened to me? Why I am so weak?'

The girl nodded. 'It was loss of blood, ma'am. He reckons you will be up and about as soon as you replace what you lost with drinks and such.'

This made sense. It had probably taken Joe some time to fetch assistance. 'How long have I been unconscious here?'

'Two days, ma'am, and we feared for your life.' The girl held the glass of barley water to Sarah's lips and she swallowed greedily.

'Am I allowed to eat? I would dearly like something small, perhaps some toast?'

'I'll fetch some immediately. Mrs Murphy is the cook-house-keeper here now that Mrs Siddons has gone. She's been asking every time I go down what she can prepare for you.'

The door closed softly behind the girl and Sarah realised she had not asked the name of her temporary maid. This was all so confusing. She was an ordinary young woman from an ordinary home and didn't expect to be treated like gentry – not even by a kitchen maid.

It was easier to think with her eyes closed and she needed to make sense of what had happened. The only explanation for there now being a housekeeper, maids and curtsies was that she had misunderstood her grandparents' situation. Could it be that they were not tenant farmers at all, but owned the farm outright and all the land that surrounded it?

Now she came to think about it, this house was in excellent repair as were the barns and outbuildings. The labourers she had seen were stout and healthy, and apart from the half-starved cat they had taken in... Good heavens! The boys hadn't mentioned Smoke – she would have to ask if the animal had been adopted into the new regime.

19

Alfie wasn't sure which train Sarah, the boys and Robert would be arriving on so couldn't really walk to the station and meet them. He'd banked most of his money, just keeping in reserve what he needed for everyday things. Ma was happy to take care of the household expenses but it were a man's job to provide for his family and the sooner he found himself something to do the better.

He took Buster for a long walk along the edge of the river, not tidal like the Colne, and it didn't smell too good neither. He decided to wander past the station just in case his family arrived on the next train.

'Alfie, I hoped you might come to meet me,' Robert greeted him enthusiastically – but his friend was alone.

'Where's Sarah, Mary and the boys?'

'I didn't see them – I spoke to Mr Siddons. It seems she had a fall in the yard and, although recovering, isn't able to leave her bed at the moment. I don't know where the boys were, but Mr Siddons didn't suggest I look for them.'

'That explains why she didn't reply to my letter – I'm sorry you had a wasted journey. When will they be able to come?'

Robert shook his head. 'That's the thing, Alfie, Sarah has decided to stay where she is. It seems she has been welcomed into the family, the boys also, and according to Mr Siddons will never be in want again.'

'Not coming? That ain't right. She was right close to Ma. She would want to see her after all these years apart. That Mrs Siddons is a nasty bit of work. What did she have to say on the matter?'

'I didn't see her either. I'm sure that Sarah will write to you as soon as she's able to. Think about it, Alfie. If she stays there, she could be the sole heir to a prosperous farm. The boys will be able to attend school again, can learn to work the land, if that's what they wish to do. Why would she give that up to come and live here?'

'Being with close family's more important than money. Come and see for yourself – we've got a fine, big house, and my ma has set up as a tailor and it seems Sarah could be part of that. I don't see her as someone what sits about doing embroidery and suchlike.'

As they walked back to the shop he told his friend everything that had taken place in his absence, including the arson he'd been responsible for.

'I'm not surprised you left Colchester – Hatch will be after you. From what I've heard he doesn't take kindly to being gainsaid and you would have been an important part of his criminal activities.'

'Here we are. I brung you to the front so you could see how smart it is. We've to go in round the back, can't take Buster in this way.'

Betty greeted Robert with a hug but her happy smile faded

when she realised Sarah and the boys weren't coming after all. Ma said little but her eyes narrowed when she heard the news.

'When are you on your next ship, Robert?'

'I've got two weeks' furlough, then I've got a position as chief officer on an East India vessel trading to India. I'll be gone a year or more.'

'Chief officer? Is that a promotion?' Betty asked.

'It is indeed. I'll be second in command. If the captain became incapacitated for any reason then I would be in charge of the ship. I need to do several voyages in this position and then can apply to be a captain. I've passed all the necessary examinations now.'

Alfie slapped him on the back. 'I'm impressed, mate – you deserve it. I've writ another letter to Sarah. Could I ask you to take it out there and hand it to her? I want to be sure she knows what's what.'

'Of course, I'll hire a hack and ride out as I'm not expecting to bring anyone back with me.'

Ma finally joined in the conversation. 'I'm surprised that a seafarer is able to ride a horse. Wouldn't have thought you'd have much opportunity in your line of work.'

'Sometimes we're delayed in a port for weeks, Mrs Rand, so I have plenty of opportunity to explore the countryside and what better way to do it than on horseback.'

* * *

Alfie insisted on escorting his friend to the station and was sad to see him go. Two years were a long time and India the other side of the world – he reckoned it quite possible Robert would never see England again.

He only ever had two other friends, if you didn't count the Sainty boys he'd got into mischief with before he'd run away at twelve years of age. He'd been closest to Jim and it had fair broke his heart when he'd died from congestion of the lungs. His other mate was George Benson, the bloke what had learnt him carpentry when he was living in the same lodging house in London.

Maybe he would visit the Smoke and look his old friend up. There weren't much to keep him in Chelmsford if Sarah and her family weren't to join them – that's for sure.

* * *

The doctor, an elderly gentleman in a faded black frock coat and grey whiskers, pronounced Sarah sufficiently recovered to get up when he came the next day.

'I shall remove the sutures, Mrs Cooper, next time I visit. However, in the meantime it will be acceptable for you to rise and go downstairs. However, you must remain inside and not risk catching a morbid sore throat in this inclement weather.'

'Thank you, sir, I shall be pleased to get up. I'm not used to being confined to my bed. I much prefer to be active.'

She waited until she heard his heavy footsteps descending the main staircase before scrambling out of bed and stripping off her nightgown. Although the children had spent a great deal of their time with her in her bedchamber, she missed them dreadfully and wished to resume her duties as soon as may be.

The girl who'd been appointed to fetch and carry had been sent back to her duties in the kitchen. Being waited on was not something she enjoyed. She was not a gentlewoman but someone from the lower classes, and she expected to take care of herself.

All her garments had been laundered, dried and pressed in the few days since she had been attacked by her lunatic grandmother. Whilst she had been languishing in her bed she had had more than enough time to think about what had happened.

Despite her grandfather's protestations to the contrary, she believed him to be as culpable as her grandmother for what had happened to her and her family on their arrival. He had known they were living in appalling conditions, were working without recompense, and yet he had done nothing until his wife had tried to kill her.

There was only one reason she could think of that could explain his sudden interest in them. He wished to make sure that she made no complaint to the magistrate about the attack. Indeed, she only had his word that the woman was indeed incarcerated in an asylum. For all she knew, Mrs Siddons could be staying with friends in the village.

The children were in the front parlour and she went to join them there. Mary clapped her hands and toddled across the room calling out to her. Three boys were equally pleased to see her. After they had hugged and kissed and exchanged greetings she settled back in a comfortable upholstered chair with her daughter on her lap. John was sitting on a footstool by her knees; the other two boys were cross-legged on the floor within arm's reach.

'Tell me what has been going on whilst I have been marooned upstairs.'

Joe wouldn't look at her and the other two exchanged glances. There was something untoward going on and she was determined to prise it out of them. Eventually John spoke up.

'Mr Billings came to collect us, Ma, but Grandpa told him we didn't want to go, that we were stopping here in future. Uncle Alfie had sent him.'

Davie glared at his oldest brother. 'Our Joe said we wasn't going whatever Uncle Alfie said.'

'Why was I not told about this? I would have liked to have seen him. However, it's too late to repine. I think you were right to say we would stay here, Joe. We shall be more comfortable living in this large farmhouse rather than cramped in the cottage in Colchester.'

No more was said about this visit and she spent a pleasant afternoon enjoying the company of her children, although, if she was honest, she would prefer to have something practical to do. It wasn't good for anyone to be indolent.

The following day she was once again in the front parlour with Mary and the two youngest boys, whilst Joe was out exercising the dog. Smoke was curled up in front of the fire as if he'd always lived a life of luxury and idleness and, not less than two weeks ago, been half-starved and unloved in the yard.

Davie was at the window when he called her over. 'Look, Ma, someone's coming along the lane on a horse.'

With Mary on her hip she went to look and recognised the rider immediately. 'Davie, go to the front door at once and let Mr Billings in. Do you think you will be able to take care of his horse? It will need to go into the barn to keep warm as it's too cold for it to stand about outside today.'

'I can do that – I like horses. I ain't too keen on pigs though.'

Her grandfather had gone to the village and she was glad he wasn't there, for she had a feeling he might not have allowed her to speak to Robert.

John had rushed to the front hall and she heard him welcoming in their unexpected guest. Then he was at the door, his large frame blocking out the light.

'Sarah, I can't tell you how pleased I am to see you looking so well after your accident.'

'Come in, Robert. I shall send the boys to the kitchen to arrange for refreshments to be brought to us. I have much to tell you and I'm sorry I wasn't able to speak to you when you came before.'

Once she was settled she told him the truth behind her so-called accident and how they had been obliged to live until she had been attacked.

'I've never heard such a dreadful story. Alfie sent you a letter with money in it so you could join him and your mother...'

'Ma? My ma? I don't understand. How is she with Alfie?'

He quickly explained what had taken place after her departure and this confirmed her worst fears. 'That man has deliberately kept this information from me.' She shared her fears about her grandfather's motivations and Robert agreed she was right to be concerned. 'I wish to leave here as soon as may be. We can hardly go today, but could I prevail upon you to arrange transportation for us for tomorrow?'

'Will you be safe here until then?'

'I don't think he intends to do me harm, just keep me from reporting the attack and having that woman arrested for attempted murder.'

'If she is indeed in a lunatic asylum, then the authorities would take no further action. I believe you might be right to suspect this is another fabrication on his part. I shall depart immediately – it might be better not to come face to face with him today.'

In less than half an hour after his arrival Robert was cantering back down the lane. The refreshments arrived after he'd left but she and the children enjoyed them anyway.

Joe returned in time to eat the last of the plum cake. She explained that they were leaving and the reasons why.

'I like it here, Ma. I reckon I could become a farmer but I ain't staying here on my own.'

'I'm glad to hear it. Mr Billings has told me we will be going to live in a large house in Chelmsford and you will be able to return to your studies as there's a church school nearby. Your aunt will take care of the babies and I shall help my mother run the business.'

'I don't reckon Mr Siddons will be pleased we're going.'

'Which is why I don't wish you to mention it. We will tell him that Mr Billings came to reassure himself that I was fully recovered, he didn't stay long, and will not be returning. Is that clear?'

She didn't like to ask them to tell falsehoods, but if they were to get away safely on the morrow there was no option but to prevaricate.

The children nodded and appeared perfectly content to become embroiled in lies and deceit. Dan would be ashamed of them. Her eyes brimmed and she turned away, not wishing the little ones to see her cry. Her husband had been gone for scarcely three months, but things had moved so fast she'd not had time to grieve properly.

This was another thing she should have noticed about her grandfather – he'd not once mentioned her loss or offered his commiserations. She could not blame herself for Dan's death but she was culpable for their current predicament. If she had remained in Colchester none of this would have happened and she would already be reunited with her mother.

No – Mr Hatch would surely have noticed if all of them had tried to slip away at the same time. Sometimes things happened for a reason, and possibly these past two weeks were part of something bigger, part of a plan the Lord had for her and her family.

Joe touched her arm. 'Ma, he's coming in. You don't want him to see you crying.'

'Why not? I lost my husband a few months ago, and you lost your father, so we're entitled to shed tears whenever we wish.'

* * *

Her grandfather lost interest in Robert's visit when Joe explained what had transpired. It was Sunday the next day and it had been weeks since any of them had attended church.

'I'm feeling perfectly well and intend to take Mary and the boys to church tomorrow. I believe it's no more than a mile from here, no distance at all for a walk even in December.'

'Good heavens, child, I have a gig. There will be no need for you to walk.' He smiled benevolently before continuing. 'However, my dear, you must not venture out until the doctor has removed your stitches. I'm sure the Almighty will understand your absence in the circumstances.'

'He might understand my missing church again, but there's no excuse for the boys and yourself not going.'

'I shall go and give thanks that I have you living with me at Hockley Farm. This week I wish the children to remain with you. I don't wish to be responsible for three boys without you being at my side.'

'Very well, but next Sunday we shall attend together. Please excuse me. I must put Mary to bed and will then retire myself. Come along, boys, you might as well retire with me and not stay down here to disturb your grandfather.'

Once they were safely in their own chambers she gathered them together. 'This has worked out exactly as I wished. Mr Billings will be here to collect us whilst Mr Siddons is at church. You must sort out any small items you have that you wish to take with you. Smoke must travel in the basket and Spot will have to run alongside.'

'It will be grand being back with Uncle Alfie, Aunt Betty and little Tommy,' Davie said. 'I've decided I don't much like the countryside, Ma. I want to be back in the hustle and bustle of the town.'

Sarah found it hard to settle and kept running through what might go wrong and prevent them from escaping. She was awake when she heard her grandfather retire and decided to go down and search for the missing letter and five-pound note. These belonged to her and she had no wish to leave them behind.

Mary was sleeping quietly, the boys also, so it was safe to creep downstairs without fear of being discovered. None of the staff lived in so there was no danger of being discovered once she was safely in the small room that was used as an office.

She removed the glass from the oil lamp, adjusted the wick and ignited it from her candle. This made it much easier to see and would assist her in her endeavours. It didn't take her long to find the letter from Alfie and the money was still inside the envelope. She extinguished the lamp and crept back to bed.

The next morning they breakfasted heartily; she'd explained to the children she didn't know when they would next get the opportunity to eat. The housekeeper and kitchen maid were busy about their tasks in the kitchen whilst she and the boys slipped out of the front door.

Davie and John had been given the task of carrying the cat, Joe was in charge of the dog and she had Mary in her arms.

'We will walk towards the end of the lane. It will be difficult for whatever vehicle Mr Billings is bringing to turn without being observed from the kitchen window. I doubt that anyone would attempt to stop us leaving, but I don't wish to risk it.'

The day was cold and crisp, the sky blue and the sun shone brightly – but with no heat. They had just reached the end of the lane when Robert arrived in a closed carriage. He was sitting next to the coachman and waved vigorously when he saw them waiting.

'Good morning to you all. I'm so glad you're here. It will be so much easier to turn the carriage in the lane than in the farmyard.'

There was ample room inside for the five of them and he scrambled nimbly back to his position on the box and the vehicle rocked and moved forward.

'Spot's following. He's not stupid; he'll not get lost,' Joe said as he hung out of the window.

The cat was purring in his basket and made no attempt to escape. Sarah wasn't able to relax until they were safely on the Colchester road and a mile or two away from Great Bromley.

'Ma, what's it like on a train?'

'I've no idea, John. I've never travelled on one. We shall all discover how it feels in an hour or so.'

Joe had settled back in his corner and had closed the window. 'It's the Lord's day, Ma. Do trains run on a Sunday?'

Her stomach somersaulted. Until he'd mentioned it, she had not considered this. 'Why don't you ask Mr Billings, Joe? If you open the window and call out I'm sure he will hear you.'

Joe didn't need asking a second time; he yelled his question and Robert's answer was quite audible inside the carriage.

'No trains today, but you are to stay at my home tonight and travel first thing tomorrow.'

Sarah didn't wish to yell a response but smiled happily. 'You can come in again now, Joe, and pull up the window. It's becoming decidedly chilly in here with it open.'

It would be good to see Ada and her many children again. Ada Billings resided in a substantial dwelling by St Botolph's Priory, which was the opposite side of town to where Mr Hatch lived. It would be unfortunate indeed if that man got to hear about their arrival in Colchester and took action before they set off for Chelmsford tomorrow morning.

After all the waiting Alfie was out of the house when Sarah and her family eventually arrived. He had decided to collect the chickens on the way back from his walk along the river with Buster. His dog hadn't run off this morning, but remained at his side.

'What's up, old boy? Ain't you going to catch a nice rabbit?'

The dog wagged his tail and pressed himself against Alfie's side. This too was unusual. There were something wrong with the dog, but he couldn't investigate now that he had a sack full of squawking chickens over his shoulder.

He weren't sure exactly how old Buster was, but he had a little grey around his muzzle now, which must mean he were a good age. The animal was his best friend, and he were closer to him than anyone. It would destroy him if anything happened to his companion.

The dog perked up as they approached the back gate and rushed off in front of him. Alfie increased his pace knowing that Sarah and the others had arrived in his absence. The birds in the sack protested at the rough treatment but he didn't care – from today things would be better as they would all be together again.

Joe must have heard Buster bark as the gate swung open. Spot rushed out and the two animals greeted each other enthusiastically. Alfie grinned. 'Give us a hand with these, lad. I've been pecked and clawed something rotten.'

The boy took the other end of the sack and laughed as the irate birds stuck their beaks through the holes they'd torn. 'Cor, look at that. We've got a good lot here, Uncle Alfie.'

'Let's hope so – they cost enough. I didn't reckon to see you until nearer lunchtime. I meant to come and meet you from the train.'

'Mr Billings got us on the early one, thought it best we were away from Colchester as soon as possible. He never came with us this time, but it were easy enough to find the house with the instructions what he gave us.'

Alfie bolted the gate behind them and gestured with his chin towards the run he'd prepared for the birds. 'In there, you open the gate and I'll chuck them in.'

The resulting racket brought the other boys out to investigate. He emptied the protesting hens from the sack and then hastily latched the gate behind them. His three nephews peered over the wooden fence at the clucking birds.

'Crikey, them hens ain't too pleased to be here,' Davie said.

'They'll settle down in a bit. Help me pull the cloth across the top so they can't fly out. I'll let them free once they've got used to us.'

John beamed up at him. 'We've got a cat called Smoke, Uncle Alfie. Do you think he'll try and eat the chickens?'

'No, he'll leave them be.' He leant down and hugged the boy. 'I'm that happy you're here. You'll like your new room.'

Sarah met him outside the kitchen door with her baby on her

hip. He was shocked at her appearance. Her face was pinched and pale – how could she have changed so much in so short a space of time?

He put his arms around her and held her close not releasing her until the baby protested at being squashed between them. 'I'll not forgive myself for what you suffered, Sarah love, but things will be right now. It's grand that Ma's back with us, ain't it? I reckon the two of you will make a good living from your sewing.'

'Ma looks wonderful. I don't remember her being so pretty. I suppose the last time we both saw her she was still married to that man and grieving the loss of our little brother.' She brushed a hand across her eyes before continuing. 'I saw how you looked at me, Alfie, but I'm not unwell. I'm missing Dan and it will take me a while to get over his loss and get back to my true self.'

'What do you think of your new home?'

'It's absolutely perfect. It's as if Ma knew we would be coming to live with her; otherwise, why would she have taken on such a large place?'

'I expect she'll tell you all about it later on.' He removed the baby from her arms and swung her around until Mary was squealing.

'Give her back, Alfie. She's not used to such excitement.'

There was scarcely time to draw breath the remainder of the day as there was so much to talk about and to show the new arrivals. The boys were happy to be returning to their lessons and would be starting the following morning. Sarah and Ma had already talked about the ladies and children's ready-made garments they intended to make and sell.

There were already plenty of tailors providing clothes for men but the same could not be said for ladies' items. He would have been happy to have invested some of his capital in this venture but Ma appeared to have all the money she needed to purchase the materials and employ the extra girls to sew.

It wasn't until the house was quiet, everyone abed apart from him, that he recalled his earlier concern about the health of his beloved dog. Buster and Spot were stretched out on the flags in the kitchen and the cat was curled up between them.

He smiled. There was nothing to worry about after all, as it were obvious his dog was perfectly well. He bolted the back door and went around checking the windows was fastened safely, the fire was banked down, before collecting his candle and preparing to go upstairs. He stopped to look around the workshop.

Things had turned out all right. Sarah would get over the loss of Dan in time – he weren't worried about that. But what of him? What place did he have in this family? Somehow it didn't sit right with him that he weren't the one providing for them, that the womenfolk would be doing that whilst he had no real role to play.

He shrugged. There weren't nothing he could do about it right now – but if he couldn't make a respectable living from carpentry then he must find something else to do. Until that time he would be satisfied with his lot. He had nothing to complain about and most blokes wouldn't cavil at being in his position. He were a lucky man and no mistake.

ABOUT THE AUTHOR

Fenella J. Miller is the bestselling writer of over eighteen historical sagas. She also has a passion for Regency romantic adventures and has published over fifty to great acclaim. Her father was a Yorkshireman and her mother the daughter of a Rajah. She lives in a small village in Essex with her British Short-hair cat.

Sign up to Fenella J. Miller's mailing list for news, competitions and updates on future books.

Visit Fenella's website: www.fenellajmiller.co.uk

Follow Fenella on social media here:

 facebook.com/fenella.miller
x.com/fenellawriter

ALSO BY FENELLA J. MILLER

A Basket Full of Babies

A Home Full of Hope

Standalone

The Land Girl's Secret

Sixpence Stories

Introducing Sixpence Stories!

Discover page-turning historical novels from your favourite authors, meet new friends and be transported back in time.

Join our book club Facebook group

https://bit.ly/SixpenceGroup

Sign up to our newsletter

https://bit.ly/SixpenceNews

Boldwœd

Boldwood Books is an award-winning fiction publishing company seeking out the best stories from around the world.

Find out more at www.boldwoodbooks.com

Join our reader community for brilliant books, competitions and offers!

Follow us
@BoldwoodBooks
@TheBoldBookClub

Sign up to our weekly deals newsletter

https://bit.ly/BoldwoodBNewsletter